STRANGERS IN THE VILLAGE

Jennifer Mitchell is asked to assist with the pageant that is to take place in Stretton village. Fear strikes the villagers when a small boy is kidnapped and pretty Sue Greenacre disappears. Don Wilson, the head-master's nephew, has also recently arrived to produce the pageant, but is he what he seems? There are many who find him strangely changed from the child they'd known, and soon Jennifer is to find herself involved with this man who, like herself, is 'a stranger' in the village.

Books by Margaret Lovell
in the Linford Romance Library:

FATEFUL JOURNEY
TEACHER ON THE WARDS

MARGARET LOVELL

STRANGERS IN THE VILLAGE

Complete and Unabridged

LINFORD
Leicester

First published in Great Britain

First Linford Edition
published April 1994

British Library CIP Data

Lovell, Margaret
   Strangers in the village.—Large print ed.—
Linford romance library
I. Title II. Series
823.914 [F]

ISBN 0–7089–7526–7

Published by
F. A. Thorpe (Publishing) Ltd.
Anstey, Leicestershire
Set by Words & Graphics Ltd.
Anstey, Leicestershire
Printed and bound in Great Britain by
T. J. Press (Padstow) Ltd., Padstow, Cornwall

This book is printed on acid-free paper

Author's Note

Stretton village is fictitious but the Battlefield of Bosworth Field Centre near Sutton Cheyney in Leicestershire certainly exists. My thanks are given to the Estate Surveyors Department of the Leicestershire County Council for making the project possible and to Mr. and Mrs. Tinsley, warden of the site, and all their staff for making my visits there so pleasant and worthwhile.

1

"COME on, do your stuff, Jen, there's a man at the desk demanding some information about the Battle of Bosworth."

Jennifer Mitchell looked down questioningly at Gwen Waters from the height of the library steps. She was used to being teased about her partiality for the much maligned Richard III. Gwen jerked her head towards the table near the door.

"That one, in the anorak. I don't think he will take kindly to being kept waiting."

Jennifer climbed down hurriedly and dusted her hands on her blue over-dress.

"All right. Can you finish up here? I'll deal with him."

History wasn't Gwen's forte and it was possible that she could be more helpful than her friend. Hastily she snatched up Rowse's *Battle of Bosworth Field* and Kendall's *Richard III* and approached the long refectory table.

"Both these give good accounts of the battle, sir. I can find you Kendall's — "

"I don't want to read through whole tomes attempting to whitewash King Richard the Third, just through a concise account of the battle engagements."

Jennifer reddened at his open rudeness. She checked a tart reply and put the books down quickly on the polished oak table.

"Of course sir. The final chapters in both of these give excellent information. We also have a booklet which is on sale at the new County Council centre at the battlefield. I'll get you one."

His dark eyes flashed pointedly towards the little silver boar pendant which hung from a silver chain round her throat.

Again she flushed. He had guessed at her interest and boorishly showed his contempt for what he considered her sentimental attitude.

He was a bit like the portrait of the king he so disliked, smallish, dark, with a rather tight mouth and far-seeing eyes which appeared greenish grey in the light which streamed from the window behind him.

He nodded curtly and she left him to find the required booklet. Even the schoolchildren who flocked into the library after four and who could be noisy and irritating, deigned to thank her for her help.

Gwen Waters grinned at her in passing. Obviously she had summed him up from the start. No wonder she'd been anxious to hand him over to Jennifer. Writing out a reading list he might find useful as a follow-up, Jennifer risked a further sneer and returned to his table. He'd already taken some notes and looked up quickly but this time he was less arrogant.

"I thought you might find this list useful later. If I can help in any way please come in and ask."

He paid for the booklet and scanned the written page.

"Thank you. I see you know your references."

"It is my job, sir."

"Quite. I suppose I can't take the Kendall with me — just for the night."

"I think that could be arranged."

"Good, I'd be grateful. I am doing some specialised work."

"Yes. If I could have a piece of paper with your name and address."

He tore off the bottom of her list and wrote,

Don Wilson
Grand Hotel, Leicester.

"I shall return it tomorrow morning, but meanwhile I can get the notes I need. The booklet is fine."

She felt dismissed as he returned to his note-taking and she left. He had been as gracious to her as she thought he would be to anyone.

She was locking up. Gwen had already dashed off on a date, when the chief librarian Harry Lambert called her into his office.

"Won't keep you more than a few minutes, Jennifer."

"It's O.K., Harry, I'm in no hurry." She seldom was these days.

He indicated a chair and frowned slightly as he noted the sad weariness of her expression. Poor old Jen. She had no business at twenty-two to be carrying this weight of sorrow. He'd always considered her an attractive girl, efficient too and the two attributes didn't always go together. Now she wore her long brown hair caught back in a large slide and somehow it lacked the conditioned shine he had always admired in it. When he'd set her on two years ago he'd thought of the old song 'The nut brown maid.' Those beautiful golden tawny eyes of hers set in the really English oval face with its fine complexion were the only real claim to beauty then, they'd been vivacious, glowing with happiness but that had been before Ken's death. She was waiting now patiently for him to tell her why he was detaining her and he recollected, with a slight start, his need to explain himself. He cleared his throat.

"I wondered if you'd go over to Stretton village for me, Jennifer, to take over the branch there and the mobile. I know you can drive it. They're doing a pageant at the Centre in a month or two and we shall naturally be putting on book displays at the exhibition. I thought, too, you might like to help with the costumes and heraldry, even take part, put in your oar for King Richard."

At least there was no malice in his teasing. She smiled faintly. Everyone knew about this 'thing' she had for the king, an instinctive urge to support one so maliciously attacked by the chroniclers and playwrights from Shakespeare through the ages to the biased history books.

But what was he asking? She looked down at the hands now tight clenched on her knee. He wanted her to go and work at Ken's centre, the project which had been his dream and that others had completed. She hadn't even been to see it, couldn't summon the courage to face it. Harry knew what he was doing. He was challenging her to face life again and intimating that if she left it any longer, time would defeat her. She took refuge in excuses.

"It's nearly twenty miles, Harry. I'd have to buy a car and parking outside the flat — "

"No problem. You know those friends of mine, the Trevors? Their daughter, Ann, is district nurse at Stretton and has her own cottage. She'd love to have you share and you'd have more time to work on the pageant."

She winced. He was being brutal again. That damned pageant! She had heard nothing for weeks from her London friends but their enthusiasm about it. A full-scale epic of Richard's life and times culminating in a re—enactment

7

of the final battle on the field itself. Had Ken been here he would have lived and breathed the pageant. Now she was being gently but inexorably pushed into a position where memories would be like a cold knife thrust to the heart. Harry said quietly, "The branch is at the Junior School and there are four villages the mobile circulates. Ted Stowe's headmaster and he's a real enthusiast, up to his neck in organising the pageant. You'll have no trouble with him. When I tentatively mentioned you he was so anxious for your help."

He didn't push it any further. Without raising her eyes she knew he was staring at her intently in the effort to gauge her reaction. One part of her wanted to say, 'Of course I'll do it, Harry. Ken would have wanted it' — but the other shrank from the rawness of the ordeal.

Still he waited and she rummaged in her bag for a hankie.

"Give me your answer tomorrow, Jennifer," he said at last. "Think it over well, girl. You know what I'm thinking. It's one way or the other now. The last thing I want to do is hurt you. We, your friends, want you to live again and — "

"This could be the cut of the surgeon's knife, cleaning out the old wound. I know, Harry, but I'm not sure the patient can face it."

He rose then and went with her down the stairs. She declined his offer of a lift. She had to be alone for an hour or two at least. When she let herself into the flat she was surprised to see that her face was really wet with tears. So she was crying at last. People always said it was a good thing. The beginning of the break-through.

She made herself a scratch meal of poached eggs on toast and yoghurt but couldn't eat it and in the end she pushed it away and went into the living-room. She'd put everything away that reminded her of Ken, the heraldic drawings, the two huge rubbings they'd done together at Ashby St. Ledgers, the crude little white pottery pig he'd bought her as the nearest thing he could find to a heraldic boar. She fingered the silver one round her neck. It was the one thing she'd used continually. It was Ken's last present and pain or not she'd made herself wear it — and the stranger in the library had looked at it with such obvious scorn.

She wrenched open her top drawer and took out Ken's picture. He was brandishing a spade. He'd been on that dig at Wakefield and it was so typical she'd had it framed rather than the conventional studio portrait he'd had taken one Christmas.

She sat down and hugged it to her and the tears came freely now and she gave rein to them.

"Oh Ken, my darling. Ken, you were as handsome as the Rose of Rouen, Edward himself, golden and hearty and almost as huge. It was too cruel you should have died like that — "

Her mind had shied from the pitiful remains of that great hulk of him all they'd retrieved from the bomb-blasted pub on the edge of the Cromlin Road where he'd gone to meet another enthusiast. She didn't care whether Catholic or Protestant hands had placed that bomb and then strolled away. It had cost four lives, and, with Ken's, all that really mattered of hers.

They'd found his briefcase with the notes he'd started on the Duke of York's Lordship of Ireland and Ken's mother had sent them to her.

"Some day, Jen, when it hurts less, you'll finish that book for Ken."

But she was a coward, a traitor to his interests. She'd pushed it away with everything else and withdrawn herself from everything that had excited the two of them. The teasing went on, of course. People forget how it hurt. You couldn't prevent that — and she went on wearing her little silver boar.

Abruptly she put on her coat, left the remains of the meal on the table and caught a bus, for once on time.

Ken's mother let her in, and her face

lit up with pleasure.

Guiltily Jen went into the sitting-room, pulled off her coat and sank down on the settee.

"I'm sorry. I — I couldn't — "

"Love, we know. I didn't ring you, just waited. You knew you were always welcome. Wilf's out on the allotment."

She bustled about getting coffee. Jennifer was glad they were alone together. Her own parents had died in an accident when she was eighteen and Ken's people had taken her to their hearts. He'd been their only son and Jennifer knew her neglect of them had been cruel. They would always think of her as the daughter they'd expected her to be.

"Harry Lambert wants me to take charge of the branch library and mobile at Stretton."

Mary Sutton bent over the coffee pot, her expression hidden from Jennifer.

"And what did you say?"

"I — didn't give him an answer. I — " she took a hasty swallow of the scalding brew. "I don't know if I can. Have you both — "

"Been over? Oh, yes. It was a bad moment, the first time, but it was worth it to see what he'd accomplished. He was like an excited child when the council said he could go ahead with the plans. There's still a lot to be done, you know, but the white roses bloomed last year."

Tears started in Jennifer's eyes again and she blinked them impatiently aside.

"There was a dreadfully rude man in the library today. Ken would have made mincemeat of him." She gave a little laugh. She'd always been the excitable one in an argument, Ken the one with the hard facts, well researched, to prove his points.

"I think Harry thinks I should come out of it — now — or never, I suppose. It's a kind of a test. He's been wonderful. They all have."

"Jennifer, my dear, you know how Wilf and I love you. I've waited, not pressed things. The blow was terrible for us but you were looking for a whole lifetime together." She stopped then pressed on hurriedly "We hope, pray, that you'll make a new life, find someone — "

"Don't — "

"My dear if it means losing you, we can bear it but this will tell you if you can go on meeting old friends, rejoin the group activities — go on with Ken's work — "

Impulsively Jennifer bent and kissed her.

"You've made my mind up for me finally. I'd almost come to the decision in the flat but I'm glad I had you to myself just for now." She got up. "Can I phone Harry before I change my mind again?"

"Of course, dear, I'll just slip into the kitchen and peel some potatoes. Wilf will be starving when he comes home and you will stay tonight?"

Jennifer nodded before she hurried into the hall and picked up the receiver.

2

HARRY LAMBERT drove Jennifer over to Stretton the following afternoon. It was a glorious May day and she wound down the window and breathed in the sharp scent of hawthorn. The trees were wearing their festive light green gowns and the hedgerows showed a dainty froth of Queen Anne's lace. The sun made a brave show as they drove in and lit up the solid red brick village buildings, embracing them with an attraction all their own. Stretton wasn't the picturesque village of half timbered black and white houses beloved of tourists but the cottage gardens were bright with early flowers and most of the properties recently painted and cared for.

Harry drew up outside a small cottage near the church.

"This is Ann's place. Looks like she can do with a bit of help in the garden. I expect Ted's got all the men working on the staging and weapons."

"Is that a hint?" Jennifer climbed out and shaded her eyes against the sun. "The church looks Norman, at least the chancel does, but the tower's been added quite late."

"That observation shows a healthy renewal of your passionate interest in the Middle Ages. I think the treatment's working."

She reached over and touched his arm as he bent to open the car door.

"Thanks, Harry. I know this idea is what you really think best for me. I promise you I'll give it a fair trial. I'll help with the pageant if it kills me — but — "

"Ring me at once if things get too tough. Now let's see if Ann's at home. She told me where the key was in case she's out on a call."

As no answer came to their knock he triumphantly produced it from under the door mat.

"Hardly original," Jennifer laughed.

"No, but who's going to steal from the district nurse? She's much too important."

On the old-fashioned umbrella-stand a note was propped.

"Sorry, Harry — have to go out on urgent call. Miss Mitchell's room is at the back. Make yourselves tea or coffee. Biscuits in tin on kitchen table. Back soon."

"Well, want to go up?"

Jennifer nodded. "My cases will be in the way down here. What a grand little place."

Through the open doorway into the hall she glimpsed Ann Trevor's small sitting-room, a roomy settee, small table propped against the half open casement window, a preponderance of cushions in bright yellows and oranges, and colourful prints pinned to the white emulsioned walls.

"Very pleasant. It must be great for Ann to have her own place after those years in the Nurses' Home. Right, up we go."

He heaved her two heavier cases into the rear bedroom and Jennifer followed and put her smaller dressing-case down quickly to dash to the window. A sprawl of unkempt garden reached to a low stone wall and behind it the green slopes of Ambien. In the distance she could just glimpse the great White Boar Standard on its mast rippling in the breeze, marking the place where the king had drawn up his forces on that last tragic day.

Harry leaned over her shoulder. "It would have been a proud moment for Ken when that was first unfurled."

She blinked back tears impatiently. "I shall be fine here, Harry. It's a lovely room."

It was very small, the ceiling sloping steeply on one side. There was a small divan with a modern continental quilt in dark blue and white matching the curtains at the casement, a built in white-painted unit and a vase of lupins and early roses had been placed welcomingly on the dressing-table.

"I'll leave you for a moment to find the bathroom while I pop down to the kitchen and put the kettle on."

"You can stay — just for half an hour or so?"

"Sure, take your time."

She leaned on the sill and made herself look towards the battlefield, Ken's greatest achievement. On the day of the pageant that peace would be broken by shouts and battle cries, the pounding hoofs of the horses and over all the painted standards would re-create a scene of England's medieval splendour. She was here to make that day a success. She'd do it for Ken and, please God, in the achievement would come an acceptance.

Ann Trevor let herself in just as the kettle boiled. She was a pretty, plump girl with dark mischievous eyes. She wrenched off the nurse's cap and ran her hands through her short curly dark hair.

"Glad to see you are settling in. I'm Ann Trevor."

Her handclasp was firm, her welcome genuine and Jennifer was sure, from the first, they'd get on well together.

"A crisis?" Harry said as he opened the biscuit tin. Ann sank down with a tired sigh on one of the stools.

Jennifer wondered if she imagined a secretive, almost guilty, look, that crossed the pleasant face of the other girl.

"Not really, but it couldn't wait, though I had hoped to be here when you arrived. Is your room O.K.?"

"Great, thanks. It was sweet of you to go to all this trouble."

"Glad to have you. I told Harry I'm the sort who needs company. I furnished the guest-room immediately, couldn't wait to invite people. It's a nice little place this. A lot wants doing, of course, particularly in the garden, but you'll guess why it's difficult to get help at the moment. Anyway, I'm crazy about this pageant myself, and spend every spare minute at Ted's place helping with the costumes."

Harry and Ann gossiped brightly about mutual friends and at last he got up to leave.

"Sorry, I can't take you over to the branch. I must dash, have an appointment with the planning officer at five. Look after yourself, Jen. Ring me if anything difficult crops up. I'll see you soon."

Ann saw him out while Jennifer stacked their tea cups in the sink.

"There's a meeting of the pageant staff tonight at seven. Like to come along? The sooner you meet the crowd the better. They're a great bunch."

Jennifer hesitated only a moment. "Yes, it won't take me more than a few minutes to unpack, then I'll come down and help you with supper."

"I'll not say no. I'm strictly an egg and chips, sausage and chips gal, in spite of the dietary lectures we had."

"I quite enjoy cooking, though I'm

not that good at it — " Jennifer reddened.

"More and more I think this was a great idea of Harry's."

"Look, he didn't really lean on you to have me, did he, because — "

"No, honestly, God, I'm tired. I think I'll just rest my poor feet for an hour on the bed, I can't imagine why T.V. sees nurses as romantic. Usually they're just overweight women with bad feet."

They were working happily together in the kitchen, Jennifer cooking spaghetti bolognese and Ann tossing the salad, when they heard a clipping of platform sandals and a girl's face appeared at the kitchen window.

"Oh, Ann, am I intruding? I didn't know you had a guest — " she paused uncertainly in the doorway. Casually, but expensively dressed, she was one of the loveliest girls Jennifer had ever seen off T.V. or cinema screen. Tall, slender as a reed, with long corn-coloured hair and those almost violet eyes novelists rave about, she walked superbly, unconscious of her beauty. She suddenly felt clumsy and dowdy by comparison.

"Of course you're not. Come in, Sue. This is Jennifer Mitchell. I think I mentioned my friend, Harry Lambert, was hoping to persuade her to take over the Branch Library and Mobile. He managed it and she's going to stay with me for a while. This is Sue Greenacre, Jen. Sit down, Sue. Have supper with us?"

"May I? I'm going to the meeting. Dad's out, as usual."

"Sure. No point in dashing back to the Hall. You're safe enough. Jen cooked it."

It may have been the change of air or the sick excitement which had left Jennifer unable to eat breakfast or lunch, but she ate ravenously, enjoying her meal for the first time in months.

"I heard you were called out to Mrs. Prevot. She's all right isn't she? Not another attack? Dad said he thought he saw a police-car in their drive."

Ann poured out more tea. "Yes, one of her turns, doctor was out on a call so I went over. She's O.K. I gave her something to settle her. She should sleep for a bit. I'll go over again before I turn in."

"Poor little Chris. It must have worried him. Old Nance will have enough to do to look after the old lady. Suppose I go over and offer to take him back with us, till Mrs. Prevot's up and about again. He loves our horses and — "

"No, don't do that, Sue." Jennifer frowned, puzzled by the anxious, sharp tone in Ann's voice. "He'll be fine. Nance will manage."

"It's no trouble. Dad won't mind. He's fond of the lad."

"Yes, we all are." Ann got up abruptly and reached for the cake tin. "You might as well know now. It's bound to come out later, but the police asked us to keep things quiet. Chris is missing. The old lady received a ransom note this morning and went half out of her mind. The station sergeant called me. Naturally till they've investigated further they want to keep a low profile on this whole business. Since the police car was seen, I don't see how they can keep it dark that they've been called in. I imagine Nance panicked."

"Chris kidnapped?" Sue's lovely face was a mask of shocked disbelief. "But when — and why? Surely the old girl's — "

"Oh, I think she's what the thrillers call 'loaded', all right. He's only eight, rather a lonely child. It's a classic case. I guess he trusted anybody who offered to show him a new colt or a litter of pups. He's the third this year, as we all know."

"What did Sergeant Hadley say? Is he — "

"He's called in C.I.D. An inspector arrived from Leicester. He hardly thinks it's the same man, but outbreaks like this happen from time to time. He's inclined to think one gives the idea to others."

"Neither of the other two were returned."

"No, trouble in collecting the ransom money. Lord, it's terrifying to think of poor Chris so frightened and alone. Don't say anything at the meeting, Sue. We'll keep things dark as long as we can."

So that's why Ann had looked so concerned, almost guilty, when she'd come in. Jennifer was struck by the horror of the circumstances. Into the friendliness and peace of the village community fear had struck — with a vengeance. She knew well enough kidnapping was once more on the increase. In fact, in Italy and France the practice reached almost epidemic proportions. She did not know and love the missing boy as Ann and Sue Greenacre did, but she could feel for the stricken old lady in her agony of terror.

3

IT was obvious that most of the villagers were unaware of what had happened to little Christopher Prevot when Ann introduced Jennifer to the assembled group later that evening. The mood was one of good-humoured raillery for two of the youths were trying on their blue tights, leather jacks and salets. Peals of laughter greeted the comment from one veteran of the first world war that the headgear reminded him of his 'tin 'at'.

Jennifer stood hesitantly in the doorway of the headmaster's room while Ann laughingly pulled the salet down sharply over one of the men-at-arms's eyes. She had never found it easy to make new friends, and had made little attempt to do so since Ken died. She'd put on dark-blue tailored trousers and a checked cheesecloth blouse and

27

brushed her hair fiercely till it shone. Ann looked unfamiliar and plumper than ever in her blue denim suit. Out of uniform she looked more and more like a mischievous schoolgirl and it was evident that she was a great favourite in the village.

"Here she is everybody, our new librarian," she said turning to pull Jennifer into the group.

From a room at the back emerged the man Jennifer knew instantly to be Ted Stowe, the headmaster of Stretton's Primary School. He was of medium height, thick-set, his bushy white hair waving back from his temples.

"So this is Harry's expert. Pleased to have you with us." His hand-clasp was firm and his blue eyes twinkled with good humour.

"Harry teases me, I'm afraid. Don't expect too much," she said hastily.

"We're all amateurs, no specialised knowledge of history or drama, but very enthusiastic. Squeal if we work you too hard. Sit down and I'll get

28

you some of my execrable coffee. Ah, here's my assistant with a tray. Always comes on cue. Cliff, come over and pour some of your charm on our new library lady."

"Jen, Jen Mitchell. Well, I don't know when I've been more surprised or delighted." The newcomer put down the tray of coffee beakers and pushed his way to her, his hands outstretched.

"Cliff, Cliff Norris? Is it really you?" Jennifer stared in amazement at the tall sandy-haired man who pulled her down onto a settee, hurriedly vacated by two surprised looking youngsters.

"It certainly is. How long is it? Two years?"

"It must be. Whatever are you doing here in the wilds? I thought you strictly a town bird."

"Oh, even cockney sparrows like to spread their wings. I saw this job in the *Times Ed* and liked the sound of it. I've been here nearly six months. Ted lets me have my head and experiment — within reason. These village lads are really with it. They've taught me a thing or two." His smile faded and Jennifer noted that look of embarrassment coming she feared and hated. "Jen, what can I say? I would have looked you up but — "

"Thanks, Cliff. You don't have to say anything. I know how you feel."

"Do you see Ken's people?"

"Yes, they've been wonderful. Taken it better than I have. Harry Lambert, my boss, has forced the issue. He's sent me out here. A kind of catharsis, I suppose, you'd call it."

"We couldn't believe it. All those weekends at that dig at Baynards Castle. I never knew anybody so mad about fifteenth-century history or so bloody marvellous. We caught his enthusiasm as if it were a disease — and his work here — well. You have seen the Centre — ?"

"Not yet. I felt I couldn't."

"Saturday tomorrow. Let me take you."

Jennifer hesitated. She knew the first

30

time would be hard and she'd braced herself for the effort and had thought to be alone. She flushed as Cliff's blue eyes searched her face intently, and she nodded.

"Yes, I'd like that. I'm staying at Ann Trevor's. What time?"

"About ten? You know what I'm like at early rising. A non-starter."

"You're still not married, Cliff?"

"Still a bachelor gay. You ought to know the score, Jen. I told Ken at the time he was chancing his arm. I nearly threw down the gage of mortal combat."

Jennifer took a coffee mug as a young teen-aged girl offered it. She was grateful for the opportunity to avoid Cliff's gaze for a while. Light though his tone was there had been a relationship growing between Cliff and herself when they met at the Streatham Archaeological Society. She'd been out with him once or twice to the cinema, theatre, a show or two. She'd liked him a lot but then Ken had arrived on the scene. They'd fallen in love, almost at first sight. They'd laughed about it together. Neither had considered the possibility, but there it was, it happened. Cliff had been hurt, but had accepted the situation. She'd still met him pretty frequently on the odd 'dig' and the Society outings and he'd wished her well when she'd taken the job in Leicester to be near Ken while he worked on the battle centre project. Now it was good to see him again and so unexpectedly. He was putting her in the picture.

"I've got my eye on a deputy headship eventually. You need wide experience and this was just what I needed. You'd be amazed how modern the teaching methods are here. You have to let the kids learn at their own pace anyway, since there's too big an age range for the conventional class grouping. It seemed 'way out' at first but I love it. I may have to produce this pageant, well — I'd love to have the opportunity really, and that would stand me in good stead with the education authority so — "

She listened, smiling. The old Cliff talking. She was glad. He'd got job-satisfaction just as Ken had. Teaching was Cliff's life. He'd make a wonderful headmaster some day.

"Hello, so you two know each other."

Jennifer looked up to find Sue Greenacre smiling down at them.

"Hi, Sue. Take my seat. Still agreeable to take part?"

"Why not, should be fun." She pointed to a pile of fabrics an older woman had unwrapped on the table, "I fancy myself in one of those fairy-tale Yorkist gowns with one of those fantastic wired headdresses."

The rich materials cascaded over the table to the admiration of the women present, cloth of silver and gold, brocades in old rose, and green, blue velvet.

"The hennins aren't easy to wear," Jennifer warned, "they'll need to be correctly weighted at the front or they'll be very uncomfortable."

"Will you take part?"

Jennifer reddened. "Well, I — "

"Of course you will, Jen. I can see you as Anne Neville or Elizabeth Woodville, what about that?"

"More like Margaret Beaufort, the lady of the book. Come off it, Cliff. I'm no fragile beauty."

Ruefully, Jennifer was aware that Sue Greenacre would indeed look ravishing in the costume of the period and she'd walk like a queen too. A little stab of envy shot through her. It would have been wonderful to play Richard's queen in this pageant.

"Did you ask young Chris if he'd play one of the princes? We were talking about it today in class. By the way, have you seen him? Mrs. Prevot didn't phone to tell us why he wasn't in school today. Not playing hookey with the horses at your place, was he?"

Sue looked blankly back at him. Jennifer sympathised with her in her quandary. She was aware that the chat had died down in the overcrowded room as if everyone was waiting on the answer. As if on cue there came the sound of a car braking sharply outside with a crunch of tyres on gravel, then the slam of the car door and Ted Stowe pushed his way to the door.

"Excuse me, if this is who I think it is — "

The babble of talk was resumed as he went to greet the newcomer.

"Who's this, Cliff? The county drama adviser?"

"He's not expected, not to my knowledge anyway."

The talk was hushed again as Ted drew his visitor into the room.

"Listen, everybody. I've not been able to tell you in advance as I didn't dare to hope, but he's arrived at last. My nephew, Don Wilson. He's going to stay with me for a while — and he's agreed to be our pageant master, under protest of course. Meet your band of helpers, Don. Here, let me take that."

Jennifer stared across the room at her antagonist of yesterday morning. So *that's* why he wanted the information about the battle. He looked as sullen and uncompromising as he had then and sat down with ill grace. It was clear that he'd have welcomed an opportunity to settle in, wash and change before being catapulted into this pageant production meeting, but he surrendered his bulky holdall and accepted coffee and a chair a youngster shyly offered.

"Don's the ideal man for the job. Some of you remember he trained at the Central School of Drama and he's taught drama and movement for the last few years though we're lucky enough to find him between jobs at the moment. He's done some outdoor productions haven't you, Don?"

He nodded as he leaned back arrogantly his dark eyes scanning the room with its whitewashed walls, dark beams and the one or two excellently displayed brass rubbings.

"Yes, I've had some experience. I understand you intend to produce in less than six weeks. We'll need to have the cast decided in the next day or so." He glanced briefly at the costume materials and his eyes caught and recognised Jennifer. "Good evening. I see we have one knowledgeable member. We met yesterday in the library, Miss — "

"Mitchell. Yes," Jennifer said quietly, "I've been detailed to take charge of the Branch and Mobile here. I shall be at your service for diagrams and information. I'll sort out all the stuff we have on the period tomorrow and send for anything else we'll need."

A glimmer of a smile touched his lips. "The book list you supplied will come in useful."

"I'm glad you found it so." She knew the stiffly conventional reply was somewhat *gauche* and found herself flushing irritably under his regard. He inclined his head curtly, a gesture she thought must be habitual with him when he wished to end a conversation and he turned to his uncle.

"You seem to have everything well in hand. I take it you've a list of hopeful actors. I'll need to know which of them can ride well, then I'll hold auditions on Monday."

Jennifer stole a glance at Cliff. He was obviously disappointed that his hopes of producing the pageant had been dashed and, with it, the opportunity to impress the educational staffing personnel. It seemed, too, that what had appeared to the villagers to be an informal agreement on who was to play what, had suddenly developed into a business-like, practical undertaking. As if they, too, were aware that their days of light-hearted fun were over they began to take their leave.

Cliff walked Jennifer to her cottage gate.

"He seems very efficient."

"Not unaware of his talents either."

He grinned. "You didn't take to our producer."

"I certainly did not. Poor Mr. Stowe. I can't see them getting on too well together."

"Oh, Ted will cope. He has the charm to soothe the most savage beast. You should see him with fire-breathing parents and difficult H.M.I.'s."

"I'm sorry, Cliff. You were expecting to produce."

"Oh, I don't mind, take a whole lot of work off my hands. Give me more time for — other pursuits." The pause before the final words was intentional and she flinched inwardly. She liked Cliff but she wasn't ready for emotional entanglements yet awhile. She breathed a sigh of relief as Ann appeared, calling goodnight to Sue Greenacre who was stepping into a dark blue Daimler. She was thoughtful as Cliff took his leave and they let themselves into Ann's cottage.

4

"THE cast list's up. Guess who's playing Richard."

Jennifer balanced precariously on the library ladder as Cliff put his head round the branch room door. Her face lit up.

"Oh, Cliff, I am glad."

"No, you haven't got the point, old dear. Not me, our Mr. Wilson. It's a bit like the end of 'Toad of Toad Hall' isn't it. Produced by Don Wilson, acted by Don Wilson. Set designed by — "

Jennifer was forced to laugh in spite of herself at Cliff's comically rueful expression.

"He isn't altering the scenery set-ups."

"Oh, he is indeed, told Joe Riley he wanted to keep the platform uncluttered. I quote 'Costumes and banners are quite colourful enough to dress the stage. We don't want to make problems'."

Jennifer perched on the top step. "Poor Joe. He'll go spare. All those grey castle interiors he's laboured over. Well, what are you playing?"

"The king. Do I look like the handsome Edward the Fourth, the Rose of Rouen?" He strutted for her appraisal.

"As a matter of fact you do. You'll look splendid in those royal robes and your colouring is just right. I have to admit that Don Wilson is a bit like those portraits of Richard, dark and sad, when he isn't looking sullen."

"He said it was imperative that all those taking part in the battle scene and particularly that final charge should be good horsemen."

"And are you?"

"No — " Cliff grinned and shrugged. "I've been learning recently. I can just about stay on but I wouldn't like to cope with an excited mount."

"And our Mr. Wilson rides well, I take it."

"He didn't comment on his own competence. Of course, you mustn't doubt it. Doesn't he excel in everything?"

She laughed. "He is somewhat sickening. Well, tell me the worst. What principal role am I down for?"

"Jane Shore."

"Anyone less like the king's mistress it would be hard to find. That should be Ann's part, by rights. Sue Greenacre is Anne Neville, I imagine."

"Yes. A pity Ann won't take a principal part."

"Well, I can understand it. She says she might be called out in the middle of the performance. If she plays a court lady or villager it wouldn't put so much stress on everyone."

"Right. I'd better get back to the brats. Listen to that racket."

"You'll have Ted on your neck. Hurry up."

He turned back briefly at the door. "In spite of what you say, you *do* look a lot happier since you came here. I thought last night you really sparkled — in the old way."

She turned back to the shelves and a little thrill of pleasure shot through her. It was true. She had settled into Stretton marvellously. Everyone was so friendly. Even the rivalry over the pageant was good-humoured. Cliff wouldn't mind playing the king when his first disappointment was over. The only clouds on the horizon was her growing irritation at Don Wilson's arrogance and the knowledge that little Christopher Prevot was still missing.

The news had leaked, naturally. It had been impossible to keep such a secret in a village when everyone knew everyone else's business. Chris wasn't attending school. Why not? Mrs. Prevot, a great favourite in Stretton, despite her autocratic behaviour, was not seen out. Excuses were given. Mrs. Prevot was unwell and young Chris had been sent away to an aunt — It was Chris's friends who probed beneath the evasions and, finally the villagers were told by the C.I.D. man from Leicester. They received the news first with dazed unbelief and later with a sense of shocked horror. They closed ranks immediately to help the stricken old lady and Detective-Sergeant Hadley was promised that no-one would interfere with the police in their investigation is, while the fullest co-operation would be given. Ann continued to visit Chris's grandmother daily and was able to report that, despite a heart condition which was giving some anxiety, Mrs. Prevot was bearing up bravely.

Jennifer had promised Ann she'd call on the old lady that day with a supply of fresh reading matter.

"Keep her occupied. It's all we can do. She likes biography and historical novels. She doesn't like what she calls 'slushy romance' but I'd think thrillers are out — for the moment."

Ted's class poured out into the tarmacked school yard as Jennifer finished packing the mobile van and he came to the gate to speak to her.

"How did Ann say Mrs. Prevot is?"

"Pretty well, considering."

"Still no news?"

"None, I'm afraid. Ann says Sergeant Hadley's very cagey, but she thinks he has some lead. The longer Chris is missing — "

"Quite. The ransom money was handed over?"

"Taken to the spot indicated but never collected. I suppose someone frightened him off."

"H'm," Ted considered. "Terrifying. You think of the brutalities of the fifteenth century, but I'm inclined to think our own's as barbaric. Torture, bomb outrages, assassinations seem to be the order of the day. It seems incredible that kidnapping should occur in an ordinary quiet village like this,"

Jennifer nodded. "I imagine everyone feels like that; crimes only happen to other people, somewhere else. You don't think something like this is going to hit you, or more disturbing, that the man responsible is following a fairly normal pattern of behaviour and that those round him never suspect his involvement."

Ted sighed. "Yes I agree. We tend to see our villains very garishly painted, not as ordinary people like ourselves weak-willed perhaps, but normal enough outwardly."

"Ask Ann to let Mrs. Prevot know we're all thinking of her — praying for Chris. The children have all been very sensible, but they're all very concerned — and frightened, which is as well. They need to be on their guard. We don't want a repetition of this — or any child poking his nose into some suspicious manoeuvre and getting harmed for his pains."

Jennifer called in at the post office. She'd run out of stationery and she owed a letter to Ken's parents. Mrs. Charlesworth, the post-mistress, was running on in her usual garrulous fashion to the one customer, Don Wilson.

"You know I remember it as if it was yesterday. Farmer Rawlings, he was purple in the face and you stood there gawping with your mouth open and all the cows strolling down the street as casual as you please. And do you know what you said when he bawled at you for leaving his gate open? Cor — I thought his eyes would pop out — "

Don Wilson wore that "I'm patient with bores for only so long" expression.

"No, I can't say that I do. A great deal of water passed under the bridge since then."

"You said — " She broke off to wipe eyes streaming with mirth. "You said, 'I shouldn't worry Mr. Rawlings, a change of scene and diet does everyone good'. The funny thing was they were chewing Mrs. Plummer's prize roses. Eh, but you were a caution. That were the first time you stayed with Ted — then there was the village concert — "

47

"I shudder to think how badly I performed," he said coldly then inclined his head at sight of Jennifer. "Good morning, Miss Mitchell. I was thinking of calling in at the Branch for a word with you."

"If I can be of assistance — "

"Yes, I'm sure you can. The costume books were excellent, by the way, and that roll of honour you supplied. We can take our heraldic devices from that. I take it you are familiar with the movements of the armies on the field."

"Yes, but so are most of the villagers and the warden — "

"Always seems to be so busy, understandable. I wonder if you could be free to walk the field with me this afternoon or — "

"Yes, I can manage that, I think, about two thirty?"

"Fine I'll meet you at the Centre. Good morning." He nodded coolly to Mrs. Charlesworth and strode out.

"He's a funny one," the post-mistress

stared after him. "He used to come regular, as a youngster, to stay with his uncle. We all liked him. The things he'd get up to you'd never believe, but he was always that friendly and open with it you just had to forgive him."

Jennifer thought Don Wilson's charm and friendliness would hardly win him any medals now he'd grown up. He'd certainly changed a lot. As if to echo the thought Mrs. Charlesworth pursed her lips.

"He's certainly changed a lot, not what I'd expect him to be like." She sighed, "Oh well, all youngsters grow up and change, don't they? Seems a pity somehow. You'd think he'd remember, though, wouldn't you? My Bill used to be pals with him when he came down. He was only saying last night that Don didn't seem to want to talk about the old days, nearly cut Bill dead, he did, seems as if he'd forgotten him — or just didn't want to know."

"Odd." Jennifer peered out of the glass sectioned door as Don Wilson walked purposefully towards the school house. "People usually like to talk about the great times, when they were happy and carefree."

"Take that concert now. He didn't act in it. The Dean's wife had got him down for an angel. He went and got hold of Gabriel's white night-shirt and dyed it red. You should have heard the fuss. He never even turned up on the night, daren't I suppose. My Bill was the other angel. He was that mad. I had to laugh. He *did* look funny with his wings and halo. Anyway it was a good thing Gabriel was able to wear young Don's costume. Now, what was it you wanted, love?"

Jennifer was thoughtful as she put the van into gear to drive up to the Prevot house. It was extremely odd that Don Wilson should not remember such an exploit, the sort of trick he'd have regaled friends with for years and considering he was now in the theatrical business. She wasn't surprised he'd not been delighted to meet his old friends again, that was in character — yet was it? Somehow the boy Mrs. Charlesworth had talked about bore no resemblance to a younger Don Wilson. What did Ted Stowe make of the changes success had made to his nephew? Ted was so utterly unpretentious that Don must be irritating him to death.

Mrs. Prevot greeted her graciously. The Moat House was a fine old property and though the moat which had given it the name had dried up years ago, a dry ditch still surrounded it. Glancing round at the high-ceilinged hall with its dutch-styled tiled fireplace, Jennifer imagined it a hundred years ago, cared for by a dozen or more servants. Now Nance, who did most duties of housekeeper and companion, ushered her into the sitting-room.

"Good morning, my dear. Please sit down. Ann told me you'd call. I'm afraid I don't get out much these days and I'll be glad to have some new books to read." She shook her head at Jennifer's unspoken question.

"No news yet, I'm afraid. Sergeant Hadley was round earlier. It seems they've discovered that a dark green car was noticed driving fast from the village on the night Chris was taken — in the direction of Ashby, they think, but no-one remembers the licence number unfortunately. There seems some argument about the make, not that I'm surprised. I don't know one from the other either. I can recognise Rolls Royce, of course, who wouldn't — and a Mini, and my own little Morris Imp. That's about as far as it goes. I don't even drive that much lately, too much traffic on the road."

She reminded Jennifer of photographs of Queen Mary, a stately tall woman in her seventies, wearing a fine, elegantly cut wine dress. She chose her books with a minimum of fuss and enquired about the progress of the pageant.

"I do hope it goes well. I'm sure it should. Ted Stowe is such a dedicated man. Chris adored him — respected his mind — " Her voice faltered a little "Pray God he's back with us in time to take part. He wants to be Prince Richard, the younger of the princes in the Tower, you know. I said I shouldn't like to be in the scene where they were smothered, but he tells me, Mr. Norris says the newer history books tend to disregard that tale. There's no real evidence against King Richard the Third. I can only say that in my young days he was considered the typical wicked uncle without a qualm about killing the children — " Her voice trailed off and she rose and went to the window. "Dear God, I can't believe anyone would kill a child — for gain."

It was difficult to know what to say. Jennifer made the usual conventional comforting phrases but they sounded unconvincing even in her own ears and she was glad finally to make her escape from the house of sadness.

5

IT was a hot afternoon and Jennifer leaned drowsily against the stile. It was so airless that even the great boar standard hung limp against the flagpole. She was startled by a sudden pounding of hoofs and for one moment it seemed that the years had rolled back and the dark-haired figure riding confidently down Ambien on the powerful white horse was the dead king himself; then she realised that it was Don Wilson. He held in his mount skilfully and dismounted near the stile.

She came towards him and fondled the big horse's nose. His rider patted him approvingly.

"He's like White Surrey resurrected."

"Not as big as a true destrier, but he'll do. The young woman at the riding school wanted to be sure I could manage him before she'd agree to my using him for the charge. He's skittish but he'll own me as master before the big day."

"Then you do intend to re-enact the battle scene? I thought you intended to use the arena and just ride off — into the sunset."

"Yes, that was suggested and I considered it but the battle actually took place here and I felt that would be a dreadful anti-climax. No, I thought we'd do the drama scenes in the early afternoon, break for tea then the spectators can gather down here behind this barrier and we'll do the final scenes. It should work." He frowned, scanning the gentle slopes of Ambien. "The responsibility is heavy, of course."

"Responsibility?"

"Of ensuring no-one is hurt, particularly the children."

She was faintly surprised by the remark, as if only the success of the performance mattered to him.

"Shall we walk?" He tethered his mount to the fence patted him again and they moved off together. He frowned as they stood beneath the standard, staring down the slope where the last tragic decision had been made.

"I can't really see why he did it."

"Ride for Henry's standard, you mean?"

"Yes. From the books you supplied it seemed as if he must have known the venture was doomed from the start. He could have escaped from the field. It would have been wiser and he had the chance of returning to fight another day."

She nodded. "He was in a terrible emotional state. He'd lost his wife only four months before and his only son not long before that. Whatever Shakespeare said I believe he loved Anne very deeply."

He glanced at her sharply. "You sound as if you speak from experience. You've lost someone recently?"

"My fiancé, only three weeks before we were to be married."

"An accident?"

"I don't think I would call it that. He was killed in a bomb blast in Belfast."

"I'm sorry." His tone was abrupt and she sensed his embarrassment.

"This battlefield project was his dream. He worked as the historical adviser with the county architect."

He glanced at her silver boar. "His interest then was — "

"In Richard, the King. Yes. He was researching for a book on the Duke of York, Richard's father who was Lord Lieutenant of Ireland. That was why — he was there."

He made no further comment and they spent the next hour moving to the various sites and discussing the dispositions of the 'armies' in the coming performance. They stood together at the spot where the king was thought to have been killed, ringed about by enemy men-at-arms like a boar at bay.

"I was unpardonably rude to you in the library."

She smiled. "It's nothing. It happens sometimes. We get used to it."

"Nevertheless I apologise." He frowned again in concentration.

"You see him as a tragic hero?"

"No, simply as a man of his times, ruthlessly cruel when he had to be but misunderstood and deliberately maligned by the Tudors for political purposes."

"And the murder of the princes?"

She shook her head. "I don't know. There is simply no proof. You talked about responsibility just now. He had the responsibility of England and there had only just been a disastrous period of civil war due to the accession of a boy king. I believe he was a family man, fiercely loyal to his brother."

"'Loyalty Binds Me', his motto."

"Yes. I can't believe anyone would do such a crime. A child — " She broke off as she had been about to mention little Christopher Prevot. His

58

grey eyes bored into her strangely and she shrugged off the rest of what she was going to say.

When they once more reached the stile the horse whinnied in greeting.

"Do you ride, Miss Mitchell? You seem fond of horses."

"I am and, yes I do."

"Well?" He had a disconcerting habit of barking out direct questions.

"I can stay on over fences."

"Then you hunt?"

"No, I disapprove of blood sports. I — we — used to belong to one of those societies which re-enacts battles. I didn't take part in the encounters, of course, but I rode with the armies."

"Side-saddle?"

"Of course."

"I chose Miss Greenacre for the principal role as I was assured she was an excellent horsewoman."

"Sue will be marvellous, I'm sure. She looks the part."

"She'll be adequate, when I've finished with her."

She laughed. He was so like one of those arrogant Svengali-type film producers she'd read about.

He laughed with her and it lit up his dark, clever face.

"Will you ride with me sometimes — ?" He paused deliberately for her to supply him with her first name.

"Jennifer. Yes, I'd like that."

"I'll ask Ruth Clements to find you a suitable mount. Tomorrow? What time will you be free?"

"In the afternoon, if you are. During the early evenings I take the Mobile round. More people are in then."

"Fine. At the riding-school? Two-thirty?"

She nodded and stood back while he mounted.

She went back to the Centre to change some of the pictures and period books in the display cabinets, then drove the van back to its garage near the school. Outside Ted's cottage a red Marina was parked and Don Wilson emerged from the house and stopped at sight of her.

"Finished for the day?"

"Yes." She stared at the car, puzzled. It had briefly crossed her mind, when Mrs. Prevot had mentioned a green car that she'd remembered Don Wilson drove a dark green Renault. Why then had he changed suddenly for this one — or was this Ted's?

He noted her surprise.

"I drove to London yesterday to the theatrical costumiers. I wanted to discuss the armour. The damned clutch went on me. A friend lives in Kensington. I borrowed his. Fortunately he doesn't drive much. He finds it almost impossible to park in London. He'll collect mine when he comes to the pageant."

"You were lucky it was available." She thought her voice sounded oddly shaky.

"I invariably get what I want. Tomorrow?" He got in and slammed the car door.

She parked the van and let herself into Ann's cottage. As usual Ann was out and Jennifer set about preparing her meal. She banged about almost fiercely, attempting to take her mind off her frightening thoughts.

On the field she had felt a growing awareness of Don Wilson and she did not think she was imagining his deepening interest in her. She had undergone a strong, compelling desire to make him believe, as she did, in the worth of the man he was to play in the performance. It was important to her that Don Wilson should understand her motives. She had been flattered and delighted, when he'd asked her to ride with him.

Now — two thoughts kept pushing insistently into her mind. Mrs. Charles-worth, the post-mistress, had found the headmaster's nephew strangely changed, so much so that he failed to remember those events which would have imposed themselves strongly on a young mind. Could he not be — Don Wilson? The thought was ridiculous. If so, why should Ted Stowe introduce him to the villagers as his nephew?

How conveniently he had disposed of a dark green car when the police were so obviously likely to interview the owners possessing vehicles of that colour. She was glad when Ann came in to dispell her rising suspicions with her usual disarming chatter.

6

IT was while Ann was checking her bag ready for her evening calls that Cliff came. Jennifer's mind was racing with the day's problems and she failed to take proper notice of what either of them was saying but she was recalled to sudden attention by a sharp exclamation from Ann.

"That's odd. I could swear I had six with me."

Cliff had wandered into the kitchen where Jennifer was completing drying the dishes. There was a rehearsal meeting tonight at Ted's.

"Something wrong, Ann?" Jennifer hung up her apron and nodded her thanks to Cliff who was stowing cups and plates into position on the Welsh dresser.

"I could swear I had six hypodermics when I packed my bag this morning."

Jennifer went back into the sitting-room. She saw at once that Ann was genuinely worried.

"You're sure you didn't use an extra one or — "

"They're disposable things at least four were, and two others, I used one disposable on Ted."

"Ted?"

"Yes, he's a diabetic. Didn't you know? I called there at lunch-time. He's well stabilised now of course but we do regular check-ups and I gave him his insulin injection, though he usually does it himself. I didn't use another today so there should be five left, three disposables and the other two. One of those is missing."

Cliff walked quietly to the table and glanced at the contents of Ann's bag laid out expertly for her consideration.

"You couldn't have lost one. I take it you never leave your bag unattended."

Ann shook her head. "Never. I always take it with me. It's not wise to leave it in the car. I rarely leave it out of my sight and today I — " She paused, frowning. "Now I come to think of it, it was — at Ted's. That little Gray girl fell down in the playground. The dinner lady asked Ted to come. We thought she might have broken her ankle. Since I was at the cottage I went with him to have a look at her. It was all right, just a bad sprain, but I did leave the bag open on Ted's sitting-room table."

"Were there children about? They go out into Ted's cottage occasionally on errands."

"I don't think so. It's possible." Ann looked as worried as Cliff. If one of the younger children had seen the bag, its contents might have proved a fascinating temptation. Little girls, particularly, loved to play at hospitals. She made a second, hurried examination to ensure that none of her drugs were missing.

"A child would surely not take a hypodermic syringe." Jennifer could think of no reason for such a theft. Rather, a child would be wary of 'the needle' as they always termed it.

"Oh, I don't know. They love jabbing each other. They've a morbid fascination for such things," Cliff said. "Ask them to mime or act a nurse and it's always an injection they show you."

"It couldn't do any harm, surely," Jennifer said, mainly to allay the mounting concern she saw in Ann's expression.

"Well, providing they only used water, but if they tried injecting other substances — well, you never know. I should have been more careful."

"Don't worry, Ann. Ted will see to it that the offender owns up and coughs up," Cliff said with a grin. "You should see Ted on one of his investigations. Everybody's made to feel guilty and sooner or later we find the culprit."

"I was only gone a minute or two." Ann began to repack her bag. "If it isn't found I must put in a report to my supervisor. It's just possible someone outside saw the bag on the table and came in — youngsters, drugs — "

"Any known addicts in the village?"

"Not to my knowledge, Cliff, but — "

"Was Don Wilson in the cottage at the time?" Jennifer surprised herself by her question and found both pairs of eyes surveying her oddly.

"I don't know. I didn't see him. He might have been upstairs, why?"

"No reason," Jennifer coloured hotly and tried to cover her own embarrassment. "I meant that if he was there no one would have had the opportunity to slip in."

"Oh, I see." Ann nodded. "I'll ask him if he was there, he'd have heard someone come in, wouldn't he? In the meantime I'd better check back on my tracks. It's just possible I left it somewhere else though I'd swear I didn't."

She was clearly worried still when she left and Cliff shook his head puzzled.

"Poor old Ann. She's worrying herself to death. It shouldn't have happened to her. She's so practical and competent. Ready?"

Jennifer nodded and picked up her jacket.

"Yes. I'd better take this. It's warm tonight but Don might want us to go to the Centre."

As they walked the short distance to Ted's cottage her mind shied from the insistent fear which jarred at her peace. Kidnappers often used drugs to subdue their victims and such drugs were usually injected. Had someone seen an opportunity to help himself to a syringe, laid out so conveniently for him to take? She told herself, fiercely, that she'd watched too many T.V. thrillers but the certainty could not be avoided. The syringe was missing and from Ted's cottage —

"Hey, Jen, you seen miles away. You haven't heard a word I've been saying."

She jumped guiltily at Cliff's somewhat aggrieved tone.

"I'm sorry. I was thinking of something."

"Something very important by the signs."

"Cliff, what will happen to Chris? It's days now since we heard anything."

"The police know what they're doing. They usually get their man in the end."

"Yes, but afterwards. Often it's too late — " Her voice trailed off miserably.

"Do you think we haven't all thought of that? It's not that we don't feel for that poor woman in the Moat House, love. This going on normally, the pageant and everything, it's just that we *have* to. Nothing would be served by not doing."

"Mrs. Prevot knows that, Cliff. I keep thinking about that hypodermic syringe."

He stopped and stared at her, his eyes widening in shock. "You think its loss could be connected with the case?"

"It's possible if the child is being kept under sedation."

"That thought hadn't really occurred to me. But Ann says she lost the thing at Ted's. Seriously — "

"I wasn't thinking about Ted."

Cliff gave a soundless whistle. "Wilson? It's just possible he's on drugs or mixed up with someone who is. You never know with a stage crowd, especially students, but the child — " His voice took on a graver tone. "He's a stranger to the village. He arrived co-incidentally at the time when — " He gave a forced laugh. "Damn it, Jen, I don't like the fellow but the idea's ridiculous."

Jennifer nodded. She did not add that Don Wilson's strangeness had been noted by one or two villagers who'd known him well previously. She tried to shrug off her uncertainty.

"What were you saying just now?"

"Oh, that? Yes. We're taking the kids to Twyford Zoo tomorrow. Why don't you come too? It would be fun. Ted thinks it's a great idea. You could help us, especially with the little girls."

"Oh, Cliff, what a pity I didn't know earlier. I can't, not tomorrow."

"Why not? You can leave the Branch work for an hour or two can't you? Watching them with the animals should enable us to get some insight as to the books we can introduce to them about the animals and the area."

"It's not that, Cliff. I've promised the afternoon. I'm going out, I'm afraid."

"Can't you change the arrangement?"

Jennifer reddened. She felt acutely uncomfortable. She had no wish to break her appointment. She wanted to ride with Don Wilson, needed to be reassured by his presence, experience more strongly the growing sympathy between them which she had felt begin earlier today, but she had no wish to hurt Cliff. He had to be told, though.

"I promised I'd ride with Don Wilson. He will have ordered my mount. We thought we might look at some of the battle terrain. If I'd known earlier — "

His face seemed to whiten in the gathering twilight.

"I see. Obviously it can't be helped. I should have asked you before but it wasn't until this morning I broached the idea with Ted that you should accompany us."

"It was a kind thought, Cliff. Perhaps next time — "

"Yes, of course."

Ted greeted them with mock anger. "Where have you two been till this time? We were about to send out a search party. Don thinks he'll have to make one or two cuts to the script and he needed everybody here before he could make a start." He checked at sight of their expressions. "Anything wrong?"

"No, of course not." Jennifer forced a smile. She would leave Ann to take up the matter of the hypodermic with Ted. Strictly speaking the matter was none of her business.

Right from the start she was conscious that Cliff was staring at Don Wilson with an intentness Jennifer found disturbing.

Don put them all through their paces. He was an exacting taskmaster. Few of the actors came off lightly. Time before the performance was short now and he had scant patience. Cliff came in for a blistering attack.

"No, no, man," Don said testily, "you're playing Edward the Fourth not Henry the Eighth. More dignity needed, and a suggestion of cold brutality even with his women. Edward was an extremely brilliant statesman and so, on occasions, ruthless to the point of cruelty."

Jennifer did not escape criticism.

"You hold yourself badly. Jane wasn't royal but women walked well then, they *had* to in those clothes. God help us all if it's too hot on the day. In these velvets and armour we'll fry."

Jennifer noticed that he was gentlest with Sue Greenacre. Considering that the girl was concentrating less than half of the rehearsal, Jennifer thought she came off pretty lightly.

"Not too bad, Sue, but remember towards the end that Anne was a desperately sick woman trying to hold off the knowledge of her approaching end from a loving husband. Good, you've caught that mood well."

Indeed, Sue didn't look well and was clearly preoccupied.

Ann, who hurried in later, whispered to Jennifer that she thought Sue was fretting over little Chris.

"She was devoted to the child. He was constantly over at the Hall. He loved their horses so."

Jennifer could tell that Cliff was trembling with anger when he seated himself next to her during the short break Don allowed them for coffee. He passed no comment about their producer, but she thought he was very close to boiling point.

The flare-up, when it came, was hardly unexpected. Don had been pushing Cliff all night. Now, in the king's big scene with Jennifer as Jane

Shore, his mistress, he called irritably to them to stop.

"Hell, no. It's all wrong. I think this is impossible. Better for us to cut the scene entirely. Cliff, you're playing the part as if Edward was a genial buffoon."

"Perhaps it could be that we've a court jester for a producer."

Everyone fell into embarrassed silence and all eyes turned on the pair who were sizing up to each other like two fighting cocks ready for action.

"It's typical for an amateur to be unable to accept criticism." Don turned his back on Cliff with an off-hand shrug.

"Why you — " Cliff sprang on him like an infuriated mastiff. Startled, Don fell back under the onslaught. Jennifer moved to try and get between them but Ted pulled her sharply back.

"Leave them alone for the moment. You'll do no good, only get hurt."

The little group of actors drew back bewildered as the combatants heaved and wrestled, each attempting to get the better of the other. It was an undignified spectacle and Jennifer was close to tears of concern and anger. How could two grown men behave so. She was aware that Cliff's fury had been roused well before he had been baited at the rehearsal. His anger at Don Wilson was far greater than the provocation merited. He had considered his interest in Jennifer inviolate and now the same pattern of behaviour that had occurred in London was repeating itself. Another had come on the scene and snatched at the prize he had thought to be now well within his reach. Jennifer felt badly about it. She had not given Cliff cause to believe she cared deeply for him, not now — or earlier, when she'd met Ken. She blamed herself for ever agreeing to go out with him, but to have refused an old friend would have appeared churlish at the time of their meeting again so unexpectedly.

Though considerably less powerful Don Wilson was giving as good as he got. It was clear that he knew how to take care of himself.

Jennifer turned appealingly to Ted.

"Stop them, they're making such fools of themselves and someone might get badly hurt."

"Cliff. Don." Ted's voice rang out authoritatively. "Come on, now. This isn't the way to settle your differences. Neither of you is a child. Break it up now."

Stung by Ted's reference to childishness, Don drew away putting up his hands to ward off his opponent. He was breathless but undefeated.

"Steady, steady, man. Ted's right. Let's call a halt. This is getting — beyond a joke."

Panting with his exertions, Cliff crouched opposite him regarding him balefully. A trickle of blood oozed from a cut near his right eye and there would be a livid bruise on Don's cheek later. How battered and stiff both would feel in the morning was obvious to the watchers. Cliff made no reply to Don's demand for a truce. He continued to crouch there, his breath rasping painfully. Suddenly he lunged forward with a lightning movement of his right fist. Don, not expecting the blow, fell back, hitting his head against Ted's heavy mahogany side-board, the only piece of furniture nearby. Everything else had been moved to allow more space for the rehearsal moves. There were startled gasps from the others and a little cry from Sue Greenacre.

Without waiting for condemnation, Cliff flung out. Jennifer heard the outer door slam hard as he left. She ran to Ted who was assisting a shaky Don to stand up.

"It's all right. Don't fuss. I'm O.K. I'm sorry, everyone. It was my fault. I'm used to working with professionals. I should have been more tactful. I asked for it." He winced sharply as Ann dabbed at a bruise on his forehead with dampened cotton wool. "Thanks. I'm lucky we have a nurse on hand." He felt his front teeth gingerly. "Looks as if I might lose this one. Damn. I'm unashamedly vain about my teeth."

Jennifer helped Ann clean him up as Ted saw the others out.

"Sorry, everyone. I think we'll have to call off work for tonight." He grinned. "Well, we can't complain that it was a dull meeting."

They went quietly enough and Jennifer knew they were a good-natured bunch and unlikely to gossip outside their own, group or castigate Cliff, once over their first shock at the proceedings.

She looked anxiously at Ted.

"Do you think I should go after Cliff or someone else — " she added hastily.

"Better not. He'll be hating himself enough as it is." Ted looked down wryly at his nephew. "I take it you don't intend to press an assault charge?"

"Of course not. I've told you, I realise it was partly my own fault. I'm pressing everybody much too hard. We're short of rehearsal time."

He stood up, gesturing to Ann his

gratitude for her ministrations.

"The only worry I have is that Cliff might refuse to play King Edward." He grimaced as he reached the doorway. "Then we should really be in the cart."

7

JENNIFER heard Ann speaking to someone as she let herself out of the cottage early next morning. She poked her head round the door before leaving.

"Gentleman to see you, Jen. Is he to come in? He assures me he is truly repentant."

Jennifer went hurriedly to the kitchen door.

"Cliff?"

"Yes. Can I come in?"

"Of course." She untied her apron and led him into the small sitting-room. "How are you feeling?"

"Pretty badly. Oh, Jen, I am sorry. I just lost control. I had to try and see you before I reported for work, if I dare, that is. What Ted will say I dread to think."

"Not very much, if I'm any judge.

Have you time to sit down for a few minutes? Ouch, that eye looks bad. Got any raw steak?"

"I've already tried that. I'll have to tell the children I walked into a lamppost." He grinned sheepishly. "I don't think they'll believe me and I don't blame them."

"I can't see their parents gossiping much about it to them. You don't need to worry."

"Oh, no? What about Mr. Wilson? He could prefer charges, if he'd a mind to."

"He's already said he wouldn't."

"So it was in his mind?"

"No, Ted asked him with a view to persuading him not to take any further action, I'm sure."

"Is he badly hurt?"

She chuckled, couldn't resist it. "I think you've loosened one of his front teeth and he's not a bit pleased about that. Come to think of it, it won't enhance his appearance on stage one bit."

"Lord, I'm sorry."

"Well, he admits he asked for it. He was rough on everyone last night, except Sue Greenacre."

"I thought she seemed a bit off."

"Ann thinks she's worrying about young Chris. Apparently they were very close."

Cliff nodded. "We're all tensed up. Last night's criticisms were the last straw. Do you think I should offer to resign the part?"

"Heavens, no. Don said it was the one thing he was afraid of. We'll all have to go on, Cliff. We can't let the village down now. It's far too close to production."

"He's right, of course. I *was* hamming it. I'd got other things on my mind."

She made no reply and he read her silence as confirmation of his worst fears.

"Jen, there isn't any hope for me, is there, never was?"

"I'm sorry, Cliff. I like you a lot, but — "

"Can't love me." He moved away, angry with himself, to stand gazing out of the window across to Ambien, his shoulders hunched. "I should have known. If it doesn't work out right the first time, it's hardly likely to later. If there'd been any real chance for me, Ken wouldn't have swept you off like that. Now — " he turned, peering anxiously across to where she sat in shadow, "Is it Don Wilson, Jen?"

"I — I don't know, Cliff. I really don't know."

He sighed deeply. "I'll have to go. I'll be late and I told you we're off to the zoo this morning." At the door he paused with his hand on the door knob. "When you talked to me yesterday, about — I mean when you and Don were alone did he say anything which gave rise to your suspicions — those mentioned last night?"

"No, certainly not." It came out in a little rush and Jennifer hurriedly lowered her gaze. "But the affair of the missing syringe came later."

"But you don't think of something like that out of the blue. It's true Don's new to the village but — "

"So am I."

"So why — ?"

She hesitated, unwilling to broach the matter of the car or Mrs. Charlesworth's opinions, for what they were worth.

Cliff's eyes were troubled. "Jen, I'm sure you would never have voiced your doubts unless there was something more to go on — because — because I think you care for him in spite of yourself."

She shook her head, a little bewildered. "Don't press me any more, Cliff, not now."

She sat on for a few moments, her thoughts confused and unhappy. The phone rang and she hurried to answer it.

"Is that Nurse Trevor?"

"No, sorry, she's already gone out on her rounds. Can I take a message for her when she drops back? This is Jennifer Mitchell. It's Mrs. Prevot, isn't it? Aren't you feeling well?"

"I'm quite all right, my dear." There was a slight pause and the old lady continued. "I just wanted her to know the police have traced the car. I know how anxious she's been about every development in the case."

"The green one?" Jennifer strove to keep excitement from her tone.

"Yes, no lead, I'm afraid. A commercial traveller came forward in answer to the police appeal. He was just passing through on his way south. The police appear to have eliminated him from their enquiries."

A great feeling of relief washed over Jennifer and her hand tightened on the telephone cord.

"I'm sorry. It doesn't seem to help."

"Well, Sergeant Hadley still seems optimistic. I try to keep up my spirits."

"I'm sure. Can we help at all?"

"I don't think so, my dear. Let Ann and Mr. Stowe know, will you? Everyone in the village has been keeping an eye open for that green car and it seems pointless now."

"I'll pass on the message."

Mrs. Prevot rang off and Jennifer finished tidying up the cottage, then went to her work in the Branch room.

It was warm in the afternoon but there was a pleasant breeze blowing which freshened the atmosphere when she arrived at Stretton riding-school for her appointment with Don Wilson. He hadn't arrived yet but Jennifer was greeted warmly by Ruth Clements, the riding instructress and proprietress of the stables. Ruth was a tough, sturdy woman of late middle age, her pleasant face lined and tanned by her outdoor life.

"I didn't know you could ride. Here she is, Amber, quite mettlesome, but Mr. Wilson seems to think you'll manage her. He instructed me to find you a spirited animal. He'll be riding Prince, as usual." She'd already led out the big white horse and it was saddled ready for Don.

Jennifer ran an appreciative hand

down the satiny neck of the chestnut mare. "Oh, she's beautiful. Yes, I'm sure we shall do fine."

The riding mistress watched as Jennifer mounted and walked her mare quietly round the yard.

"Yes, she'll suit you well, I reckon. You'll be riding in the pageant, then?"

"Well I doubt it. There's no call for Mistress Shore to ride really — "

"A pity. You'd make a fair showing side-saddle, I understand. Young Sue's not too used to that. We've had to send for one for her, borrowed it from a friend of mine. She's riding in the coronation royal progress scene." Ruth Clements narrowed her eyes against the sun to peer at the big white gelding. "Funny when you come to think of it. Young Don, he was right frightened of horses in the old days. Ted brought him over for lessons, but I could never get him to feel confident, never thought he'd stay up for a trot, let alone a gallop over fences." She grinned broadly. "And

I thought I could pick 'em, men and thoroughbreds but you never know, do you? Here he is at last."

"My apologies, Jennifer. Good afternoon, Mrs. Clements. I'm sorry to have kept you waiting. I've been in to Leicester."

They walked their mounts out of the village and let them have their heads in the near-by country park. At length Don drew rein as Jennifer galloped up to him. His eyes passed approvingly over her bright yellow sweater and jodhpurs to her fingers, capable on the reins.

"You do ride well. You don't overestimate your abilities."

"Did you suspect that I did?" Jennifer was stung to irritation and he laughed.

"No, but my standards may well have differed from yours. I've a favourite clearing down this ride. Shall we go?"

She followed and he helped her dismount. They tethered their mounts to low-hanging branches and sat down together on a fallen tree-trunk. Only feet away from them a little stream bubbled its way over stones and around a small otter dam. Jennifer smoothed back straying tendrils of side hair. She'd tied the rest back with a brown silk chiffon scarf.

"You should really be wearing a hard riding hat."

"I know. I haven't mine with me. I borrowed the breeches from Ann but if I'm to ride regularly I'll have to go into Leicester and get my own things."

"You live alone?"

"I've a flat there, yes."

"I'll drive you in, tomorrow, if you like. I keep having to go over for materials and paints. I'll need tons of silver and gilt spray. I've ordered some more at the suppliers."

"So that's where you were."

"Yes." He looked away from her briefly. "I trust Mr. Norris is in a better mood today. I saw him go to your cottage this morning as I drove off."

She smiled. "He's quite repentant. He should be. He's got a lovely black eye. How's your tooth?"

"Oh, pretty well, I think. I saw a dentist in Leicester and he appears to have made an excellent job of fixing it."

Her eyes sparked mischief. "Fortunate. A missing front tooth could radically affect your diction."

"I'd have had .to have it crowned, but that takes time. Is all your concern for the success of the pageant only? You wouldn't have wished to see King Richard leering villainously over a gap in his front teeth would you?"

"I'm sorry. I shouldn't have sounded so unsympathetic, but you were a brute last night. As you yourself said, you rather asked for it."

"Did I?"

She found his direct gaze disconcerting and tried to avoid it.

"Well — "

"I think there was more to Cliff Norris's anger than wounds to his pride as an actor. You told him you'd been with me alone yesterday afternoon at the Centre."

"Yes."

"He resented that?"

"He didn't like it."

"There's an understanding between you? I don't know how else to put the question."

"No. I'm fond of Cliff. I knew him when I was engaged to Ken. There was never anything serious going for us."

"He accepts that?"

"He does now."

Don nodded. "This has all been difficult for you, working here. I understand your fiancé was a brilliant man. Memories must be very painful. You loved Ken very deeply. No doubts?"

"None at all. Ken was everything to me. We seemed set fair for a whole lifetime — " She swallowed hard. "It's over. I have to face that. I'll never forget Ken but he's gone and I have to learn to live without him, courageously.

I think this has been good for me, coming here, I mean, and working on the pageant. My boss thought so, that's why he sent me."

"And young Norris thought — "

"I think he hoped." Jennifer felt herself flushing hotly. "It's difficult. I had no cause to snub him, yet — "

"Very difficult," Don agreed, dryly.

She thought it best to change the subject.

"I had a phone call from Mrs. Prevot earlier. It seems they found the driver of the green car and have dismissed him from their list of suspects. He was just passing through, I gather. One thing out of the way, but it doesn't take the police any further."

"No, it's a very nasty business."

"Do you think — ?"

He looked away across the stream. "We have to face facts. Kidnap victims rarely survive. Is the old lady very wealthy?"

"I wouldn't have thought so. Like you, I'm new to the village so

I don't know a great deal about her. Ann says she's heard the boy has some money in trust, but they seem like a typical 'country squire' family. Nowadays kidnappers go for the children of wealthy industrialists or political figures. It doesn't make sense. That child must be going through hell."

He rose and stooped to help her up. "Fortunately children appear to ride these crises pretty well. He's probably finding it all quite an adventure."

"But he may be badly treated."

"I doubt that. It would make him difficult to handle and, for the present, the boy is necessary to them. My guess is they'll keep on the right side of him, till — "

Jennifer flinched from the implied thought and walked soberly to where Amber was contentedly cropping grass.

"All this could kill Mrs. Prevot. I pray the police get those responsible quickly and put them away for the rest of their lives."

"Rather cruel. Don't you think life sentences are more extreme than executions? Imagine those poor devils without hope."

"I'm too busy imagining that little boy bound and gagged somewhere and terrified," Jennifer retorted.

"It bears out my opinion. Women can be heart-whole in their hating."

She took the reins from him and wondered what experience he'd had of a woman who'd detested him so thoroughly that he'd deemed it 'hate'.

8

THE talk the following night before rehearsal was about the elimination of the prime suspect. Pete Lawson, the vicar's son, was indignant.

"They just don't seem to be getting anywhere. I think experts from the Yard ought to have been called in by now."

"I imagine they've called on all the reserves of central C.I.D. What could a Yard man discover that a local man, with background knowledge of the area couldn't?" Ted said quietly. "I'm sure everybody's doing his best. Sergeant Hadley doesn't seem to me a man who'd overlook any possibilities." He looked quickly towards the door as Cliff entered and there was a little embarrassed silence. One or two of the members of the company looked awkwardly at the dark mauve and yellow bruising round Cliff's eye and tried to pretend they hadn't seen it. Pete Lawson made room for Cliff beside him on the settee.

"Hello, Cliff. Have a good day?"

"Great, thanks." Cliff's eyes found Jennifer's and he nodded a greeting. "Where's our producer?"

"Here, Norris. I was just finding some sketches of armour for you all. I'm glad you've arrived. We can get to work right away. Has anyone seen Sue Greenacre? I'd like to run over the scene where Richard discovers that his brother, the king, is dead."

Mary Lewis who was putting the finishing touches to Sue's costume shook her head.

"No. She promised to come over this afternoon and try this on. She didn't ring me to cancel so I stayed in, waiting. In the end I thought she might have had a headache or needed to go into Town for something. Did she ring you, Ted?"

"No, that's odd. She's usually very punctilious about things like that. No side to Sue. I've never known her to let people down or just take things for granted."

Don shrugged, "Perhaps the car wouldn't start or she's torn her jeans or something. She'll turn up, I expect. We'll run through the lines of the Tower Council scene while we're waiting. We'll go into the schoolroom. I shan't be wanting you women for the moment, so you can go on with the sewing if you like."

Jennifer stopped Ted as he moved to go with the others.

"I'm short of jewels for my hennin. Didn't you say you'd get some broken beads I could have?"

"Yes. They're upstairs in the attic. I'd better come up." He hesitated. "Oh, perhaps not. Don wants me, I know. I don't think you'll have to move any heavy cases. There's a brown trunk near the little window. I keep a lot of junk in there. I remember seeing some dress brooches and earrings in a blue cardboard box. Someone gave them to me for school plays. Take anything you like. You'd better bring the box down. I imagine they'd be useful for quite a lot of you."

"I'll manage, thanks, Ted." She turned on the second step, "You don't mind me rummaging among your things?"

He laughed. "Nothing private up there, my dear. I threw out all incriminating love-letters a long time ago."

It was gloomy in the tiny room, light filtering in only faintly from the small square window. When Jennifer's eyes grew accustomed to the light she located the old trunk and thrust back the lid. Kneeling down, she gently felt about until her fingers encountered the cardboard box Ted had mentioned and lifted it out. Almost immediately she realised that it must be the wrong one for there was no sound of beads rolling about as she expected. However she could find no other box so she opened it wondering if the contents had been wrapped tightly in tissue paper, so preventing the pieces from clinking against each other.

The box was filled with old photographs and faded snaps. Hurriedly she made to put back the lid when several fell out onto the wooden boards. Ted had said there was nothing private here but she felt she must hurriedly replace the snaps in the box, unwilling to pry into what must be intimate glimpses of Ted's family life. One fluttered out of reach and she had to search among the cases and piles of books until she found it. It had fallen face down and bore a boyish scrawl. The name 'Don' caught her eye and she was unable to resist the temptation to look at what must be a picture of Don as a boy, on one of the occasions when he'd come often to stay with his uncle.

Certainly the youth, pictured in cricket whites, brandishing a cricket bat purposefully and grinning into the camera view-finder, bore little resemblance to the Don who was now ruthlessly putting his cast through their paces in the schoolroom below.

Jennifer sat back on her heels and lifted the snap so she could get a better light on it from the window. The youngster looked as if he might be dark, as Don was, perhaps tallish, but then she didn't know his age when the snap was taken, but there was something about the pose which was utterly unlike Don Wilson.

This boy was clearly self-conscious, and his attitude was unnatural, theatrical. Jennifer couldn't imagine Don, even at the gawky, awkward age, ever standing so 'placed'. She thought if he had agreed to be photographed at all, it would have had to be snapped, as he played, without falseness of stance or deliberation. She turned over the snap to examine the writing, over-large and boyish.

'All I want for Christmas is my two

front teeth'. The first line of an old song, and beneath, 'You can see the damage done in last week's match against Desford. I'm getting my wired ones on Saturday'. Then there was the scrawled, 'Don' and the date 'June 5th, 1963'.

She peered again closely at the face. It was just possible to see the gap, which gave the boy a lopsided ugliness that was attractive in its youthful honesty.

But Don Wilson *hadn't* lost his two front teeth. The thought struck her with the force of a blow. Only this afternoon he'd told her that the dentist in Leicester had been able to 'fix it' without crowning and last night he'd shown definite anxiety lest the loosened tooth should have to be extracted. This boy was waiting for a small dental plate. He must be all of fourteen when the photograph was taken, so, undoubtedly, it was his adult teeth which had been struck by the stray ball in the village cricket match — so how could he have grown new ones? All Jennifer's doubts crowded back. The man who was producing this pageant, the man she'd ridden with this afternoon, was not Don Wilson. It was impossible. Yet why was he masquerading as the headmaster's nephew? Ted must know, and, if so, why was he, too, deceiving the villagers?

Mrs. Charlesworth had said he didn't remember events of his boyhood. Ruth Clements, the riding-school instructress, said her Don Wilson had been afraid to ride.

There could be no doubts. The newcomer was being shielded by Ted — and deliberately. But who was he and why should he wish to live here in Stretton under an assumed name? If she challenged him with her suspicions he would deny the deception and Ted would support him. For the present she must keep quiet, watch and wait.

When she put back the box in the trunk a linen bag next to it gave a betraying clink. She untied the string round it and saw the gleam of coloured beads. Thank Heaven she could return with what she'd gone for and would not need to ask Ted further questions. As she descended the stairs her thoughts returned to their conversation by the stream. Don's sympathies, curiously, had seemed to be partly with the kidnappers. Certainly he wasn't unduly concerned about the missing child's state of mind. Yet he had calmly faced the stark ugliness of the possibility of murder.

Jennifer gave a little gasp of horror. The very doubt was unthinkable. The man she had ridden with, talked with twice, as she had never done with anyone since Ken, was surely incapable of — yet there was a mystery and she must not let herself become emotionally involved until she knew the truth. Ruefully she acknowledged the fact that detachment towards Don Wilson was virtually impossible.

Mary exclaimed over the collection of old necklets and brooches. Some of the stones could easily be prised from their settings and would look really effective on the costumes while others could be sewn on just as they were. Ann had now joined the sewing group and they all bent over their respective tasks. Jennifer carried her headdress to the light to try against it a handful of heads. They were jarred from her hand as the door was thrust open suddenly and Sue's father, Sir Hugh Greenacre, stormed into the room. The women stopped their chattering to stare at him wonderingly. It was evident he was under great stress.

"Where's Ted?" he said abruptly.

"Rehearsing in the big schoolroom. I'll fetch him." Sandra Rawlings, one of the youngsters, scrambled up awkwardly and hurried out.

Ann had come in and was drinking coffee in the doorway from the kitchen.

"Is anything wrong, Sir Hugh?" she said quietly. "You seem upset."

He was a tall man, of military bearing with the small neat moustache so popular in the thirties and forties.

His proud, upright figure seemed to crumble suddenly as Mary insisted on him sitting down.

"It's Sue, she's missing. My last hope was that she'd come here to Ted or was with one of you." He gave a short barked laugh. "Quite idiotic, of course. Her bed wasn't slept in. She's been gone since some time last evening, obviously."

"What's this, Sir Hugh?" Ted checked, his tone astonished as he came in followed by the anxious youngster, who peered white-faced, from behind him. "You say Sue hasn't been in home today? We're sorry. She isn't here. We were all wondering why she hadn't turned up for rehearsal."

"She didn't come for her fitting this afternoon, either," Mary said quickly.

Ted moved to Sir Hugh's side and sat down on the edge of the settee. It was clear that the man was near to collapse.

"Ann, get Sir Hugh a brandy, will you? You know where it is. I was about to ring you, but you know what girls are, I just thought for once, she'd found something more to her taste for the evening, a sudden meeting with a boyfriend, an unexpected invitation she didn't want to turn down. Sure it isn't something like that?"

Sir Hugh took the brandy glass, Ann offered and drained it gratefully. His hands shook a little as he returned it.

"I don't think so, Ted. That fool housekeeper of mine didn't tell me till just now that her bed hadn't been used. Said she hadn't wanted to alarm me. I expect, like you, she thought Sue was out with some fellow last night and that discretion was the watchword. I didn't see Sue at breakfast this morning but she often gets up at the crack of dawn and goes riding, used to with young Chris — " His voice trailed off uncertainly and he wiped the sweat from his forehead with the back of his hand. He pressed on more firmly now. "I had to go out on business, had lunch with my accountant, so it's only now that — I don't believe Sue would stay out like that. Even if she had, she'd have given me a ring this morning. It's damned worrying, Ted, after this other business. You can't help thinking — "

"Have you phoned the police?"

"Haven't liked to. I mean she's over the age of consent — and — "

"Quite." Ted considered. "Sandra, ask the boys if they'd come here for a minute, will you? Tell Mr. Wilson Mr Stowe thinks it's urgent. He'll understand if we make a short break." As the girl hurried back he explained, "Pete might know something. One of them might have seen her yesterday after rehearsal."

"I saw her about half seven," Ann said. "She was going towards Mary's cottage. I thought she was going to try on the costume. I was on a call so had no time to chat. I shouted from the car and she waved back. Then I saw her later at the rehearsal of course."

"She seemed all right. Happy

enough?" Sir Hugh was eager for any crumb of information.

"Yes, perfectly O.K. She wasn't dressed to go out. Jeans, her green sweater. I tell you I thought she was on pageant business either to help the boys paint the shields or to Mary's."

"When was the last time you saw her yourself, Sir Hugh?" Ted asked.

"Oh about six, I think. We had tea together and she said she probably wouldn't be in for dinner. She was always having scratch meals in the village with her friends. I don't wait up for her. Who does, nowadays? I tell you it wasn't until Mrs. Chater came to ask me this evening if I knew whether Miss Greenacre had gone up to London or was just away for the weekend that I realised it has been some hours since anyone in the house saw her. She couldn't have come in last night."

"Odd." Ted considered then nodded, relieved, as the men came in. "Good, here they all are. Lads, Sir Hugh's a bit worried about Sue. Who saw her last night after we broke up here?"

"She was with us till about ten," Pete Lawson said. "We all went to 'The Sun' about that time for a bite and pints."

"She was helping with the scenery?"

"Appliquéing designs on the standards."

"But she didn't go with you to the pub?"

"She was going to, then she had the phone call and said she had to leave."

"Phone call, here, in this cottage?"

"Yes, just as we were packing the stuff away we heard the phone ring. You and Don were at the Centre. Sue said she'd come and answer it and it was for her. I thought it was you, sir." He nodded towards Sir Hugh.

"How did you know it was for her?"

"She said so, Ted. We thought at first it was for you, naturally, and that she was taking down a message."

"Oh, so she wrote something down?"

"Yes, tore the top sheet off the pad. I remember because Bill lent her his biro. She said the one on your desk wouldn't write."

Sir Hugh looked blankly at Ted. "Mrs. Chater says there *was* a call for Sue about nine. Presumably she told them she was likely to be at rehearsal and gave your number."

Ted went to the desk and picked up the small white jotting pad used to note down appointments and messages. He carried it to the window and held it up close to the light.

"No indentations I can see. One of you, give me a pencil." He scribbled furiously for a second or two then shook his head. "Nothing. She must have torn off the sheet underneath, possibly more than one."

"Then that would indicate the fact that she wished no-one else to see the information her caller gave." Sir Hugh half rose, excitement audible in his tone.

"Oh, not necessarily. Sometimes two or three sheets come off at once, accidentally. Nothing ominous in that. I just thought we might have got some clue as to where she went when she left the lads."

"She'd hardly go off to meet a boyfriend in Leicester at that time, dressed like that," Ann pointed out.

"I don't know. Anything seems to go, these days," Ted said grinning broadly. "In my young days a girl wouldn't. If she were invited to dinner at nine or ten she'd have dashed home to dress for it or declined, but today, well — " He shrugged expressively.

The little company had fallen uncomfortably silent. Jennifer stole a glance at Don who leaned against the door-post. Ted caught her look and turned to his nephew.

"You didn't say anything unduly harsh to young Sue last night, did you?"

Jennifer recalled that, in fact, Don had been unduly patient with Sue and she wondered why. The girl had seemed to have something on her mind. She'd been very half-hearted about her performance.

"I didn't speak to her after our slight — contretemps." He smiled towards Cliff who reddened.

"Oh, she wasn't upset about the rehearsal, I'm sure of that," Pete said hastily. "I mean we were all talking about — " He broke off awkwardly. "Sorry, Cliff, but well, you know — She didn't pass any comment. She seemed very intent on the job in hand. When I asked her how she fancied herself in that luscious gold brocade gown she didn't seem to have heard me. Not like old Sue. Clothes were her abiding passion."

"Sir Hugh," Ted said, "I should ring Sergeant Hadley, just let him know the situation. Did you try the — "

"Hospitals? Certainly. I rang every one of them within an area of thirty-mile diameter. No admissions by that name nor indeed anyone unidentified who could remotely resemble Sue."

"Well, that at least is a blessing. I shouldn't worry about consulting the police. They'll be very discreet, especially considering the circumstances in this village. Your main problem is that they're unlikely to consider Sue as a missing person until she has been away some time or — or until you receive some indication to the contrary."

Sir Hugh nodded. He got up from the settee like a really old man and Jennifer's heart bled for him. He could not be blamed for fearing the worst. It was in the mind of everyone present.

"Thanks, Ted, for your advice and understanding. If any one of you hears anything — " His eyes roved the company and dwelled in particular on those of the younger members of the cast.

They all nodded in answer. As he reached the door Don Wilson said curtly, "I take it you checked to see if your daughter packed a suitcase."

It was so cruel, cutting across the cocoon of sympathy which surrounded Sir Hugh, that Jennifer caught her breath at its brutality.

Sir Hugh turned and confronted Don. "Yes, Mr. Wilson, I did," he said. "None of Susan's clothing has been taken. I would hardly have panicked or burdened you all with my problems without first dismissing the normal reasons which would take a young girl so hurriedly from her home."

He drew himself up again, assuming his former dignified bearing, and withdrew, Ted accompanying him to the cottage gate. There was a little hush and then the chatter broke out again.

"I don't get it. People like Sue just don't walk out," Pete said half angrily turning accusingly towards their producer.

"One can never gauge the strangeness of people or the sudden pressures that force them to hurt others who love them," Don said evenly. "I don't think we'll get much more done tonight. Can two or three of you help me put back the desks and tidy up in the schoolroom? We'd better call it a day."

Pete hesitated then gestured to two of his friends and they followed Don across to the school building. Cliff came over to Ann and Jennifer.

"We *do* seem to be seeing life since we engaged on this pageant. Poor Sir Hugh. It's a very worrying situation. I think I'll leave young Pete to help Don out tonight or I might say more than I should. Good night, everyone."

Ted was quietly thoughtful as he saw his guests out. As they walked the short distance to Ann's cottage, Jennifer asked her what had clearly been in Don's mind.

"Do you think she ran away from home, Ann? You appeared to know her pretty well."

"I can't believe she did. Mind you, she hasn't always seen eye to eye with her father."

"How long is it since Sue's mother died?"

"Oh, years. I don't know exactly. Sue was a very little girl. She's been away at school over the last few years. The last one was in Switzerland. She came home finally at Easter."

"And boyfriends?"

"You can see what it's like. The local fellows flock round her like bees round a honey-pot. Natural enough. She really is lovely."

For the first time since they'd met, Jennifer thought she detected a slightly envious note in Ann's comment, but in a second the young nurse had dismissed any jealousy for her friend's success with the opposite sex from her mind. "She's a wonderful person, too. There's always been money, plenty of it, but she's not spoilt. There's an element of sound practicality in her make-up. I've never known her show off and, truly, I think she's never really realised how pretty she is."

"Then she *could* have been kidnapped — like Chris."

Ann inserted the key in the lock. "I don't think Ted's dismissing the idea," she said soberly, "and heaven only knows he's not one to let his imagination run away with him."

9

THE branch room door was flung abruptly open the following lunch time as Jennifer was completing her selection. The children had been dismissed and she expected it would be Cliff who wanted her but it was in fact Don Wilson, who peered up at her as she balanced on the steps.

"You always seem to be up there whenever I need you."

"Won't be a moment. Just the last of these romantic novels and I'll be with you."

He took the heavy pile from her, waited while she picked up her tray of tickets and stamp, and followed her to the outside door.

"Have lunch with me." It was more of a command than an invitation and she hesitated.

"What's wrong? Is Ann expecting you?"

"No, I'm going to have a scratch meal but — "

"Fine. then you can come." He slammed the doors of the van and stood back while she locked up. "My car's ready."

"Car?" Her tone echoed her surprise. "Aren't we going to 'The Sun'?"

"We are not. For once I want something more substantial than a ploughman's lunch and infinitely more appetite-titillating than bangers and mash." She climbed into the passenger's seat and fastened the belt.

"I take it you've sampled Ted's school meal."

He shuddered and turned the ignition key.

Jennifer was startled however when half an hour later he led her into the very elegant dining-room of what seemed to be a very well-appointed country club.

"Don, I'm not dressed for this. I

thought you knew of another pub where lunches are a speciality. I'd never have agreed — "

He glanced appraisingly at her simple cotton dress with its white trimming.

"You'll do. You can remove the book dust from your hands in the powder room. I'll give you five minutes."

"Thank you very much, kind sir. On your head be it if that supercilious waiter suggests we should both be more formally attired."

He shrugged, indicating complete unconcern of the waiter's opinions, and she retired to tidy up. As she had expected he'd ordered for both of them when she got back to the table.

It was an excellent lunch well served and she stirred her coffee thoughtfully afterwards. Not once had he mentioned why he had summoned her.

"I take it this is a business lunch?"

"Oh?" He raised one eyebrow, then sampled his own coffee.

"Brandy, sir?" The attentive waiter hovered at his elbow as he had throughout the meal.

"Not when I'm driving. The wine was excellent and sufficient. Jennifer?"

"Thank you, no. The meal was perfect. I've everything I want."

The waiter accepted his dismissal and moved off.

"It really has been a wonderful meal," she said warmly. "I've enjoyed it even more because it was so unexpected."

"I'm glad."

"Are you a member here?"

"God, no. I'm not the sporting type. Ted is. He rang through and made the arrangements."

"Just on the spur of the moment."

"Certainly,"

"He must be very used to your sudden whims."

"Oh, he copes."

He had not risen to her bait and she decided to probe no further into his relationship with Ted Stowe.

"You did want to ask me something."

"Yes, I want you to take Sue's place in the pageant."

123

She gave a little gasp and her hand jarred the coffee cup down on the table.

"No — I couldn't."

"I don't see why not."

"But we don't know — " she floundered wildly. Her one secret desire had been to play the part of queen to Don's Richard. Now she felt appallingly guilty that her wish had been granted so unexpectedly and in contradiction to her longing. "She might be back — It was only last night that we heard. Don, I couldn't. It seems so heartless to replace her so soon."

"I don't think she'll be back in time to rehearse. That last time she was dreadfully weak in the part. We have to be practical. Dress rehearsal is very close and Mary will need to adjust the costumes. You are our only hope."

"You criticised me — strongly, and then I was only playing a minor part — "

"It is pointless to criticise unless one detects the possibility of improvement.

I saw none in Sue's performance."

"I don't look like Anne Neville."

Again she flushed under his cool scrutiny. "I think you do — or *will* do. After all we have no portrait of Anne to guide us, only the Rous drawing, and that could resemble anyone. I think I can make you give a fair performance."

She was rattled by his arrogance.

"Not nearly as good as your own — but adequate. Good enough for an undiscriminating audience."

He frowned in surprise. "We aren't professionals. I won't flatter you, Jennifer, even to please you. That isn't in me."

She checked her rising fury and stared at him bewildered. Was this last statement a betrayal of his very real interest? She was very close to tears and did not know why. Could she blame Don for her own feelings of conscience? She had wanted him to notice her. Only with him did she have that glorious release from the dull ache of loneliness which had been with her continuously since Ken's death.

For days she had tried to thrust back the knowledge of her own commitment but it was impossible. She was in love with Don Wilson, even though she could not trust him, and his latest piece of cruelty was like a barb in her wound.

"Last night you were so sure Sue had gone off with some man. How do you know that even now the police haven't found her body in some wood?"

"I don't, but I hardly think it likely either. Oh come, now, Jennifer, why this dramatic pessimism? The girl's pretty and nubile. It's more than likely she's off with a boyfriend. Her whole lack of attention the other night indicated that."

"You're a great judge of a woman in love I suppose."

He shrugged again lightly. "They do appear to behave in a logical sequence of patterned behaviour."

"Would you be kind enough to drive me back please?" It was a childishly stiff request but she could hardly walk back. It would be all of thirteen miles and she knew, to her cost, that bus services in the vicinity were almost nonexistent.

He nodded and summoned the waiter. She silently waited while he settled the bill and followed him back to the car-park. Neither spoke during the drive and he drew in opposite Ann's cottage. He reached out and prevented her as she moved immediately to climb out.

"Do not think I am not as worried as the rest of the village about Sue and the child. The point is the pageant must go on. That's show business. I've known actors do Hamlet while a wife or child is dying."

"And you would applaud that?" she shot back at him. "I happen to think he'd be better at the bedside."

"It's a matter of opinion. An actor has to consider the rest of the cast. In a professional company if a star withdraws, often the show folds and everyone falls out of work. Have you any idea what a disaster that is in a world where work is hard to find?"

"This isn't a professional performance. No one will lose financially."

"Are you suggesting that we cancel the performance because two of the company are missing?"

She looked away from him. "No, but — "

"You are the only person to take Sue's place. There isn't time to consider. I want you to think about it then turn up prepared to play Anne Neville at tomorrow's rehearsal." He reached across and opened the door. She scrambled out and hurried into the cottage.

Ann was coming out of the kitchen as she tore up the stairs.

"Anything wrong?"

Jennifer made no reply and she followed her up and paused in the doorway of Jennifer's room.

"Have you had lunch?"

Jennifer had collapsed onto the bed

and her answer was muffled.

"Yes, thanks."

"Was that Don's car?"

"Yes. He took me to some country club."

"Oh, great. I wish someone would take pity on me and give me a slap-up lunch." She peered closer. "You all right? Have you had a row?"

"He wants me to take Sue's place."

"Oh." Ann considered and sat down beside Jennifer on the bed. "Well, I suppose he has to think quickly. We're so near production."

"Ann — it seems so heartless."

"Why? Sue wouldn't want the whole thing scrapped whatever the situation."

"Is there any news?"

"No, nothing about either she or Chris. Now come on, Jen, why the scene? You've been crying, and you're really upset."

Jennifer still couldn't face her friend. She sat awkwardly twisting her handkerchief into a damp bundle in her hands.

"I wanted to — so much. It seems dreadful somehow."

"Wanted to what? Play the part? Oh, I see. Well you haven't stolen it from her, love, have you, and frankly her best friend would have to admit she was no Sarah Bernhardt."

"Don was so unfeeling. It's clear he thinks she's just walked out with some boyfriend."

"Well, it's crossed my mind. I told you, there have been rows with Sir Hugh."

"She told you of someone special?"

"No. She mentioned some ski instructor at Saint Moritz. The school was about two kilometres from the resort. I wasn't aware that it was serious. Sue was always falling in and out of love. That's why Sir Hugh's had to keep a tight rein on her."

"But she took no suitcase, nothing."

"I know. It's puzzling and worrying but we mustn't get too panicky. In my job I learn not to."

"Then you think I should — play the part?"

"Well of course I do. Who else can?"

Ann rose and moved to the door. "Look, love, I'll have to dash, I have to dress Bob Riley's arm and give Mrs. Norton an injection. Make yourself some tea. You've the rounds to do still, haven't you?"

Jennifer nodded bleakly and Ann stared at her hard.

"You're in love with him."

Jennifer reddened and turned away.

"Is that what it is? Where's the problem? Has he got a wife and seven children?"

"I don't think so," Jennifer stared miserably at her handkerchief again. "I don't know."

"Of course he hasn't, you idiot. I checked."

"Checked? What do you mean?"

"Well, I'm not blind. I could see you were — interested, so I pumped Ted on the subject."

"You didn't."

"Of course I didn't. Credit me with some sense. Look, Jen, Harry told me the way things were. He asked me to help if I could. I don't mean to interfere or to probe. No good's ever done that way, but when I saw you with Don, well, things seemed to be working out. I was glad for you. What's the problem?"

"I suppose Ted told you all about his nephew, but he's lying, Ann. Don isn't his nephew. Can't be. We don't know who he is and what he's doing here but Ted's shielding him. I can't think why."

"What?" Ann's pleasant face registered sheer horrified amazement. "What in heck are you saying? Of course Don's Ted's nephew."

"How are you sure, because Ted says so?"

"Well, why shouldn't he be? I mean — "

"Mrs. Charlesworth thinks he's changed — a lot. He won't chat

132

with her son who used to be a bosom pal."

"Well people do grow out of friends, especially — "

"Ruth Clements says Don Wilson was afraid of horses. You rarely grow out of that and — " Jennifer took a deep breath and launched her final bombshell. "You don't grow a new set of second teeth. Your medical training has taught you that, Ann."

As Ann's bewilderment was increasing by the second Jennifer told her of her finding of the snap, among Ted's things.

"You were there. Don made a big fuss about his front teeth when Cliff hit him. I tell you, Ann, whoever he is, he is *not* Ted's nephew. Why Ted says he is I can't think but — " she faltered then pressed on, "I don't know what to do, Ann. I love him — terribly, but why is he lying to us and what is he doing here?"

"God knows!" Ann stared back at her blankly.

"You *do* believe me?"

"I have to. You've made too clear a case for us to dismiss it. Have you told anyone else?"

"I broached it vaguely — to Cliff."

"That won't help."

"I don't think it registered. He was thinking about other things at the time."

"He's jealous."

Jennifer hesitated. "He's fond of me, always has been, but he's accepted defeat, at least, I think he has."

"He could make trouble for Don — when he's had time to think about this further."

"Cliff's not malicious. Anyway, he doesn't know the whole of it."

"You're afraid Don's in some sort of trouble, aren't you?"

"I can't think why he should be hiding out here if he isn't."

"I can't believe Ted would knowingly shelter a wanted criminal."

"Unless Don has some hold on him." Jennifer turned away. "The whole idea is absurd. I ask myself where is Ted's real nephew and is he aware of 'Don's' imposture I'm so miserable, Ann."

"Of course you are. I'd feel the same. It's terrible to love a man and not be able to trust him."

"What should we do, confront Ted?"

"I don't think that would do any good. He'd deny all knowledge and we'd be forcing Ted to lie further. It must be pretty bad for him as things are."

"And Sue?"

Ann's eyes opened very wide. "You're not suggesting Don's connected with Sue's disappearance — or that of the boy? You are — that's what you're too horrified to face. Oh, no, Jennifer. I won't believe that."

"Do you think I want to, either? It's just that — the missing hypodermic went from Ted's and — did you ever find what happened to it?"

"No, come to think of it, I meant to ask Ted and never got round to it — that's why you asked if Don

135

was in the cottage." She shook her head almost angrily. "No, Jennifer, definitely, no."

"But don't you see, Ann, if we've any suspicions, now, however stupid and impossible they might prove to be, we ought to do something. This is the thought that's been tearing me to pieces since I finally found the snapshot. If we mentioned what we know to Sergeant Hadley, Don would be investigated. Even if they cleared him of any involvement in the kidnapping they might turn up something else — "

Ann nodded, her eyes, for once, shadowed with real concern. "It's a tremendous responsibility. The only thing I can suggest is that we tell Ted."

"I can't, Ann. I know I should but I can't. Last night Don was so brutal to Sir Hugh as if it was a cut and dried certainty that Sue had gone off with some fellow, then he coolly offers the part to me. No suggestion of concern about her."

"He must have his own reasons for thinking that and for being here as 'Don Wilson'. I pride myself on being a fair judge of people, Jen. I have to be, in my job and whatever pointers there are to Don's masquerade, I can't really believe he's involved un anything really shady. I think we should wait for a couple of days, until we know something definite about Sue, then tackle Ted together."

"Oh Ann, you're a great comfort." Jennifer's smile glimmered through her tears. "I do hope and pray you're right."

"For your sake, love. Now off you go with the mobile van then tell Don tonight you'll play the part. At least we can hope the pageant goes off reasonably well. It will break a lot of hearts in the village if we have to abandon that."

10

JENNIFER stood back to see the effect in the long pier glass Ted had had conveyed to the mobile dressing-rooms for the convenience of the actors during the dress rehearsals. Mary peered up at her anxiously, her mouth full of pins.

Jennifer could not suppress a little gasp of pure delight. Mary had done wonders in the short time at her disposal in altering both the fit and fifteenth-century style to suit her.

The gown itself was of old gold brocade trimmed with imitation marten fur, its high waist and long sweeping folds giving Jennifer a regality she had never thought to possess. The tight sleeves fitted to perfection and the crowning touch was given by the high hennin, surmounted by a gilt coronet and yards and yards of veiling which fell from it to the floor.

She tried an experimental walk, gathering up the front fullness of the heavy material and holding her head high as she had seen Yorkist ladies do in those wonderful illustrations of the old illuminated manuscripts; the jewels at her throat and on the velvet frontal of the hennin gleamed dully under the electric light. It was fortunate that Yorkist court ladies never showed their hair, even shaved it back to give that high brow so popular at that period. Her brown hair would not be noticeable, perhaps as well, as she thought the queen had more than likely been fair, with that red-gold tint for which Plantagenets and Nevilles were famed. She was glad Don had not insisted on carrying historical accuracy to the lengths of ordering his women cast to shave off their eyebrows.

"Excellent."

She turned hastily as she heard Don commend Mary.

"A great job. I don't think anything

needs altering for me but I think Cliff could do with a slight sleeve adjustment." Mary scurried out giving a final admiring glance at her own handiwork.

Jennifer suppressed a second little gasp at sight of Don. He was transformed. He really *was* Richard, as she had seen him in the portraits.

He wore blue woollen tights and a wide-sleeved doublet of murrey coloured velvet, the Yorkist colours. Across his shoulders gleamed the ornamental chain of uncut gems from which hung Richard's personal device of the White Boar.

He smiled at her pleasure.

"Mary's a treasure. I had not thought to look so effective — and you, Jennifer, you quite take my breath away."

"I hope you find it easier to move in your costume. However did they manage these trains over the rush-strewn floor which must have often been greasy after the banquets?"

"Practice, they were used to them

and found them less problematical than our tight jeans, I suspect."

"For all the beauty of these, our jeans are more practical and hygienic," she said ruefully.

"True, but our audience will really feast its eyes on the jewel bright splendour of these costumes."

He closed the door and came nearer to her.

"I wanted a word with you before we begin."

"Anything wrong?"

"Nothing. I want to thank you for changing your mind and agreeing to play the part — "

"After I'd had time to think — well, 'the play's the thing' as Shakespeare says. We can't let the village down now."

"You've learned the lines really quickly."

"I'm still not word perfect."

He grimaced. "Whoever is — until a run's over? No, I thought last night you were splendid, especially in the

141

scene where you receive the news of your son's death. I almost found tears in my own eyes."

"Thank you." She lowered her eyes, smoothing the rich unfamiliar material with her fingers. "I wish you all the luck in the world. Don, it *must* go well on Saturday. You deserve that it should. You've really flogged yourself this last week."

"Praise indeed. That touches me. You've been so distant lately. I thought I'd offended you."

"Of course not." She felt a little breathless. "Why should you think that? I was stupid at the Country Club. It was just that I was worried about Sue."

"Still no word?"

Jennifer shook her head. "No, nor of the boy. The police have called off the dredging operations in the county. We can still hope while they find no — bodies." She shied from the final word and he nodded. "Time's young yet, particularly in Sue's case."

"You still think she's alive and safe — ?"

"I'm sure of it." His tight mouth relaxed in a smile of encouragement. "Get it out of your head that you are taking from Sue her right to the 'so-called' glory of this performance. What I know of Sue she'd want you to do it and the pageant to be a success, whatever has happened."

"Yes, I'm sure she would."

He came close and abruptly he turned up her chin and bent and kissed her. She drew back and almost tumbled over the loose folds of her costume and he was forced to take her by both hands and steady her.

"Just for luck. Have I alarmed you, Jennifer?"

"No, no of course not." Frantically she tried to release her hands but he drew her to him.

"Now isn't the time. I know but — " He broke off as suddenly as he had kissed her, as if afraid of proceeding further. "I feel there's something between us, Jennifer, not Cliff, I'm convinced, but something more. I know I didn't make a good beginning of our acquaintanceship but — " he smiled crookedly. "I'll play Richard splendidly for you, I promise. Will that make up for my appalling rudeness that afternoon in the library?"

"Yes, of course."

"And you do forgive me for doubting him?"

"Idiot, there's nothing to forgive. Everyone must make up his own mind about the character of King Richard. You can only play the part your way, the way you really thought he would behave."

"And we'll talk further — about Richard — and other things?"

Her heart was pounding uncomfortably and she was close to tears.

"Yes, if you wish it."

Ted's voice sounded anxious outside the door. "Don? You in there? The Press have arrived. They're anxious to photograph you and Jennifer."

She caught a sudden spasm of alarm cross Don's face.

"Must they photograph me? Surely a complete cast picture — "

"Naturally they'll want one of you in the title role." Ted's voice sounded odd, tinged with some undercurrent of doubt.

"Very well. I'll change into armour. More appropriate. Jennifer you go with Ted and let them take you. No-one could look more ravishing than you do in that gown."

The next hour was one of the usual chaos of Press photography. As Don had said the young photographer whistled long and loud when he saw her and insisted on taking several studies. Finally he turned his attention to the children and she was able to relax.

Cliff, splendidly unfamiliar in scarlet and cloth of gold, came over to chat and she flushed under his candid appraisal.

"Jen, that's breathtaking. If Ken — " He broke off awkwardly.

She shook her head. "Don't be afraid to say it, Cliff. I'm over that terrible shock of grief and proud to look the way Ken would have wanted. Thank you."

"Well, there's a study for you. The war god riding to battle."

She followed Cliff's gaze to where Don rode the big white gelding into position for the photographers. Her eyes clouded as she noted the decisive movement as he lowered his helmet visor. As Cliff had said he made a poignantly heart-stirring sight in his steel armour, the gold coronet on his gleaming helm in the late sunlight. Certainly that shot would be the most effective of any, but she could not rid herself of the disturbing thought that he had chosen to be portrayed in full armour with lowered visor so that no-one would even so much as glimpse his own features when the photographs appeared in the local paper. Mentally she gave herself a shake. She was imagining things again. The choice of this shot was obvious and not everyone liked publicity.

Their exchange just now in the dressing-room had moved her strangely. She'd not allowed herself to dwell on her growing feelings over the last hectic days of rehearsals and fittings. He had made it plain that his own emotions were touched, or had he?

She found Cliff's eyes on her, watchful, and, gathering the fullness of her skirts before her, she moved towards the little knot of people who were watching the men try out the charge. Bill Norton, Mary's son, was busy with his cine camera and he called a cheery challenge to Pete Lawson, armed and wearing his helm.

"Come on, let's get some shots for the record. Head the van to the ridge of Ambien."

Jennifer saw that Don had dismounted and was moving towards the mobile changing-rooms. Ted was still in earnest conference with the reporters. She called a warning as some of the youngsters streamed onto the field.

"Be careful, Pete. Watch out for the children."

He reined in his sorrel and raised his visor.

"Hey, you kids, keep clear for a bit while we take the photographs. Anyway Don said you were to get back and change."

His young cousin, dressed as his squire, ran to his horse's head and called to one of the property boys to hand him a lance.

Jennifer moved to Pete's side.

"Don't you think you should wait for tomorrow's rehearsal when all the children are under the care of their respective leaders?"

He nodded regretfully.

"Bill, Jen's right, let's call it a day. This brute of mine's getting a bit restless."

Bill waved his camera.

"Oh, come on, Pete. I only want to shoot a couple of feet. You know what it's like. Don won't let us stop and repeat anything tomorrow. Just you and Mark and Rob and the other mounted knights."

"But by rights you should have Don leading us."

"I'll get that tomorrow. Now let me get Norfolk's advance. Rob, get your men-at-arms to advance, will you."

Rob Weston, the postman, as the Earl of Oxford, called his group to order.

"Right. Get your standards, lads, and watch how you handle them. Don will have your blood if there's any damage."

There was a lusty cheer from the older lads from the secondary school who were to form the advance force of Henry's army under Oxford.

Jennifer moved back as Pete lowered his helmet visor and moved his horse into position. It seemed a bit quieter now. For some time she'd noticed it pawing the ground restlessly and whickering. It was anxious to be off at full gallop across fields and resented being held in during the tedious moments of photographing. She looked for Cliff, feeling that someone should be in charge of the younger members of the cast, but Ted was moving back to the wooden platform stage with the two reporters. He was indicating the hard work that had gone into its erection by the youth club members and scouts under the direction of the local carpenter. He was far too busy to give his attention to the children. She called to Mary and rounded up the little ones who were eager to see the charge, herding them well back out of the men's way.

Pete was a good horseman. He signalled the group behind him with a raised gauntleted hand and the cavalry advance began. The horses behaved well, moving sedately, one or two tossing their heads and one neighed shrilly. All went well until Rob Weston's men broke cover from behind low bushes, yelling and waving their swords. Two enthusiastic archers let fly.

That did it. Pete's horse some distance ahead screamed with fury, reared and careered off across the field straight in line for the enemy, who gave way on both sides under the onslaught.

There were startled screams from the onlookers as Pete tried desperately to control his mount, then there was a soul-shattering thud as he was thrown heavily and the horse galloped off, jumping the hedge and thundering across the neighbouring barley fields.

It was just as if everyone was transfixed. For a moment no-one moved. Pete's huddled form lay some distance from the cavalry group and the foot soldiers.

Rob Weston galvanised himself into sudden action and sped across to him, followed by Jennifer who stumbled heavily over the impeding folds of her gown.

"Leave him. Don't touch him." Don's voice arrested Rob as he meant to turn over Pete's motionless form.

"Careful, there may be spinal injuries. Mary get Ted to phone for an ambulance." He had removed both his armour and helm but still wore his leather tunic and chain mail. He knelt down and examined Pete without moving him.

"He's out cold. Rob, get one of the riders to go after that horse. It will do damage and possibly injure itself. Is Ann here?"

Jennifer shook her head. "She's out on a midwifery case. Don, does it look bad?"

"He's concussed. It's difficult to say if he's broken anything. Rob, help me to turn him, very gently, onto his side. Good, he's breathing normally. Let's get rid of this helm."

Jennifer signalled to one of the boys to lend them his cloak. She removed Pete's gauntlets and rubbed his chilled fingers. Between them and skilfully avoiding all unessential movement the other two slipped one cloak under Pete's head and covered him with a fur-lined one Rob had been wearing.

Ted came up, white-faced.

"Ambulance is on its way. I phoned the rectory. The rector's out. I told the housekeeper to let him know and send him on to the hospital."

"Good." Don sank back on his heels. "We can't do anything now but wait. Will you attend to the children with Cliff? Keep them clear of the ambulance men?"

It seemed an age, though, in fact, the ambulance from Leicester arrived in record time, before Pete's limp form was lifted onto a stretcher and carried across the field to the parking place. Don followed the stretcher into the back of the vehicle.

"I'll ring you from casualty as soon as I have word." He nodded to Rob and Jennifer. "Thanks. Try not to worry. I've seen this sort of thing before, probably just bruises and concussion but — you never know."

The ambulance drove off through the group of silent, frightened spectators and Ted briskly organised the rest of the cast into the changing-rooms. Cliff came out hastily to assist him with the children.

Jennifer hurried into her own dressing-room ahead of the other women. She wrenched at the hooks of her gown and dressed quickly in her slacks and sweater. Don's room was empty when she paused in the doorway. He shared it with Cliff and Pete. An addidas type bag, she knew was his, stood under the table and she snatched up his jeans, sweater and anorak and stuffed them inside. Outside the dressing-room she found Ted.

"Have you a key to Don's car?"

"Yes, I do have a spare, as a matter of fact. He always insists I carry one in case he drops his down a drain. Why?"

"It will probably be very late when he will agree to leave the hospital. I thought I'd drive in and fetch him home. You've much too much on your plate here."

He nodded. "A good idea. I see you've got a change of clothes for him. Right, let us know how things are with Pete. I'll get back to the rectory after I've sent all the children home."

The roads were pretty clear and she made good time, parked the car across from the hospital and went into reception to enquire for Don. A young nurse pointed to a waiting-room where Don sat, his face set, looking incongruous in his strange clothing. His eyes lit up at sight of her.

"How is he?"

"They don't know yet. He's still in X-ray. They're worried about a possible skull fracture."

"Has he come round?"

"He hadn't when they wheeled him off. He's in no pain of course, one good thing."

"I'll wait here. You go in the gents and change. You can't be comfortable in that gear." She thrust the sports bag into his arms. "Besides, you're alarming the locals."

He gave a ghost of a smile and rose.

"Sensible girl. Thanks."

She sat down in his place and watched him as he walked away. His face had been one mask of fear. Surely Pete could not be so seriously injured and yet he'd taken a heavy fall. She'd read of medieval knights who had been killed by such falls in tournaments but Pete's costume armour was not nearly so weighty. The ground had been extra hard, though, after weeks without rain. She sat huddled miserably on the bench until Don rejoined her, carrying two cardboard cups of coffee.

"I wasn't sure if you took sugar."

"Thank you I don't, but it doesn't matter. It's very welcome anyway."

He sat down at her side and gulped the black coffee.

"Damn it. I shouldn't have left them alone."

"Don you're not to blame. Pete's not a child. He's eighteen."

"Excited, anxious to show off. It's

natural enough. I should have known."

She glanced at him sharply.

"That's why you insisted on playing Richard yourself, instead of Cliff. You thought it could be dangerous."

"It *is* dangerous if you're not an experienced rider, especially when the mounts aren't used to trumpets and all the yelling. I should have seen everyone back to the dressing-rooms before I changed myself."

He was taking his responsibility hard. Despite his modern clothing he still resembled the fifteenth-century king he'd been playing and the thought stirred in her that men like Don and Richard always took it hard when things went wrong, took upon themselves the blame for what was often the faults of others. Her fingers stole to touch his hand and he took hers and squeezed it gently.

"Thanks for coming, Jenny."

It was the first time she'd been called that, as if it were his own special name for her.

"Ted and Cliff were busy organising and Ted's going to see the rector as soon as he gets back to the village. He's at a diocesan council meeting. Ted's left word for him and will drive him here, unless he comes straight ahead on his own. I'm not sure if the meeting is here, at the cathedral."

Don grunted approval.

"Don't say too much to them. Rob was so keen to take this film of the rehearsal. I was worried about the children but — "

"Pete's horse had been playing up during the photographing session."

"Yes, but he was able to hold him in. I think it was the sight of that army of youngsters advancing on him. It just took fright and bolted. Pete was too desperate to keep him from injuring the lads to look to his own safety."

"The whole thing was easily enough done." Don broke off as the young surgical registrar paused in the doorway.

Don sprang up at once followed by Jennifer and they both hurried to him.

The doctor smiled reassuringly. "Nothing to worry about, Mr. Wilson. He's badly bruised and shaken up but there's no fractures."

"No skull injuries?"

"Nothing we can detect. He's come round now and he's very anxious to see you. We'd like to keep him in overnight of course, under observation. Would you like to come and have a word with him before they take him up to the ward? Not too long, mind, he's under sedation."

Don's tension appeared to drain from him immediately. "Thank God. He went with such a thud we thought he might have broken his back. His father should be in touch very shortly."

"Good. It's likely he'll be too sleepy to see him later but all being well we should be able to discharge him tomorrow."

A young nurse showed them into a curtained cubicle where Pete lay back on his pillows. His expression showed his concern for Don's temper.

"Don, I feel rotten about this. It was all my fault, I — "

"Steady." Don grinned down at him. "I shall be a damned sight more angry if you get yourself into a state now. You're a lucky devil, do you know that? You could have broken your neck."

"Worse than that, I could have ridden down some of the boys. Everyone O.K.?"

"Yes, you're the only casualty."

Pete's hands reached out towards Jennifer.

"Jen, you warned us."

"Never mind, Pete. Everything's fine. The doctor says there are no serious injuries."

Pete nodded ruefully. "As soon as I came round my main concern was for the pageant, but they tell me I should be O.K. to ride in a couple of days."

"Yes, well, we'll see how you are first. Your father should have been informed by now."

"Lord, he'll get into a dreadful state.

160

Ring through to Ted and tell him I'm fine, will you?"

"Right." Don glanced over his partially mailed attire. "We'll see you get some sensible clothes when your father comes over for you. We'd better go now, before Sister kicks us out. Get a good night's sleep."

As Don put back the curtains Pete said breathlessly, "I can play the part? You won't — "

Don turned and Jennifer marvelled at the warmth of his smile. It was rare that he did so and it transformed his usually severe expression.

"Idiot, of course you can — provided you're well enough, so just concentrate on obeying the doctors and getting out of here quickly. We need you, Pete."

Outside in reception he let out his breath in a little gasp of relief and ran his fingers through his hair.

"Thank God. I was sitting in there all that time fearing the worst. He seems all right, the young idiot."

161

Jennifer nodded. She'd gone through hell herself.

"I could do with a meal. It's late. Do you know a place which serves reasonable food at this hour?"

"Yes, there's a Chinese restaurant round the corner. It keeps open till midnight. It's quite good. We — I often went there."

"Right, I'll just ring Ted and then you can lead me to it."

11

IT was a good meal and towards the end they'd become almost gay. It had been such a relief to know that Pete Lawson was going to be all right and Don relaxed as Jennifer had never known him do before. She felt the coiled spring of tension within him had finally unwound and she felt completely happy and comfortable with him for the first time.

He drank his coffee and, turning up her sleeve, looked at her wrist watch, since she hadn't thought to snatch up his from the dressing-room table.

"I've enjoyed that and I needed it. I feel as if somebody's sand bagged me."

"It's all the worry, not only about Pete but it's been a dreadful strain trying to organise everything in the time. Do you really think Pete will be

163

well enough to play Norfolk's part?"

"I hope so, He'll break his heart if he can't, but we'll have to go by what the doctors say. It's not Pete who's worrying me now. Young Kevin Stoneley's gone down with some strange rash so we might just be without one of the princes."

"Oh, no. Has Ann seen him?"

"This morning. She says it could be chicken-pox. Fortunately he's been away from the other youngsters for a fortnight. They've been on holiday, so, with luck, we'll avoid an epidemic — until after the pageant, at least."

She chuckled. "Oh dear, Poor Don. I shouldn't think Cecil B. de Mille had so many problems as you've inherited. You must be cursing Ted for getting you mixed up in all this."

He was gazing beyond her and she detected a slight movement of the pulse at his temple as if she'd touched him on a raw spot.

"Oh, I don't know. There's nothing like work to set a man to rights and the more you worry about others, the less time you can spare for your own problems. I'll call the waiter over and settle. You must be almost all in, yourself. There'll be plenty to do tomorrow. I doubt if the property people organised everything, so we'll have the chaos of sorting everything out for the final rehearsal."

It was a dark night, past eleven-thirty, when they reached the car park. Jennifer shivered a little as she climbed into the passenger seat. She'd been racing about all day in the sun, then sweating for fear over Pete, now she pulled her heavy woollen jacket on feeling suddenly chilled.

Don touched her cheek, "Cold?"

"Just a bit. Reaction I imagine."

"You should have heard Ted's sigh of relief. He said he'd tell the rector to wait till tomorrow to see Pete." He peered at the clock on the dashboard. "Come to think of it, it's almost tomorrow now."

He drove expertly and she leaned

back in the seat pleasantly tired as they turned out of the city suburbs and his head lights picked up the dark shapes of trees and hedges and illuminated road signs. She was almost drowsing as they turned off the main road and headed for Stretton when her attention was caught by something on the road ahead.

"Don, slow down a minute, there's something in front of you, an animal, perhaps. I do hope someone hasn't hit it and left it to die."

He peered ahead, muttered a faint curse and pulled in to the grass verge.

"We'd better see into it. We can't leave an injured animal to suffer."

She was inclined to let Don do the investigating. She had a horror of seeing a mangled body and could not have brought herself to put an end to some tortured creature's suffering, but she knew her attitude to be cowardly and she scrambled out of the car to assist Don if she could.

"Jenny?" He was calling her agitatedly.

"What is it?" Her heel caught in a rabbit hole and she wrenched her foot free to reach him quickly.

She could not believe what she saw and could only stand and stare.

"Have you got some scissors in your bag? A file even." His urgent tone brought her to the need for action. "Come on, Jenny, let's cut him free — "

She dropped to her knees and searched frantically in her shoulder bag. Don leaned over the small boy he had drawn close to him and gently eased the long strips of adhesive plaster from the mouth and eyes.

"Steady now, laddie. Don't fight me. You're with friends. It's all right."

The car headlamp picked up the boy's bewildered grey eyes as he blinked from one to the other of them.

"Who are you, please?"

"The question is, who are you? Christopher Prevot?"

Don was answered by an imperative nod of the head.

"Where — where am I?"

"Quite near home. You're safe now." Don's voice was muffled as he fought with the ropes which bound the boy's legs and arms. Jennifer's nail scissors were useless to cut the thick rope but he was able to loosen the knots with them and at last the boy was free. He stood up and tried to move but the circulation had been impeded and he stumbled and would have collapsed if Don had not lifted him and carried him to the car. He placed him on the back seat, tore off his anorak and placed it round the boy's shoulders. Chris was trembling now as if with delayed shock.

"There's a brandy flask in the glove compartment."

Jennifer hesitated. "Don, he's so young."

"Just a tiny sip can do no harm. He needs it."

The boy sipped experimentally at Don's warning then coughed weakly and lay back wiping his mouth with the back of his hand.

"Oh, it's all fiery. Made my eyes water." His voice was husky with pent-up tears but stronger now. "Thank you for helping me. I *am* Christopher Prevot. I've been held prisoner for quite a long time. I'm afraid I don't know how long or where. Two men — I think they wanted money from my grandmother. She lives — "

"We're from Stretton, Chris. Don't worry. We know all about it. I'm Don Wilson. I'm living with your headmaster, Mr. Stowe, and this is Jenny Mitchell, the village librarian."

His grey eyes blinked at them again, owlishly. "Are you? I am glad to see you. Could you take me home please?"

Jennifer almost cried at the controlled dignity of his request.

"Right away, Chris, but tell me how you got here. Can you remember or were you asleep?"

"No, they didn't drug me, not this time. I was tied up and bundled into a van, I think. I'm not sure because they'd already put the sticky tape over my eyes, but I heard two doors slam, so it wasn't a station wagon and I rolled about a bit on the floor so there was quite a bit of room."

"Then they just stopped and lifted you out?"

"Yes, onto the grass verge. The older man warned me not to move about because I could get hurt. I couldn't just lie there, though, could I? There haven't been many cars but I rolled near the edge hoping someone would see me in their headlamps but I fell off the verge and then I thought I might get run over."

Jennifer bent over the back of the passenger seat and leant to touch Don's arm. He was sitting at the back with his arm round the boy.

"Don't let's bother him any more, Don. Let's get him home and let the police know immediately."

"In a minute." Don tightened his hold on the boy's slim shoulders.

"Chris, how long did you think the journey lasted and were they driving fast?"

"Not really fast. It's difficult to say, because lately every day seemed to last so long, but I'd think less than half an hour."

"Did you ever see the house where they held you?"

Chris shook his head emphatically. "Never. When they took me in, I had a hood over my head. That was nasty, and I told you they put that plaster on my eyes tonight."

"You've not been blindfolded all the time."

"No, but they hobbled my feet with rope — you know like they do ponies."

"So you didn't see out of the window?"

"I tried, but they were too high, even when I scrambled onto my feet and then onto my stool."

"Don — "

"Look, Jenny, Chris is a bright lad. He knows what I'm getting at and how

171

important it is. He's all right now for a little while."

"I'm fine. You want to trace them, don't you."

"Yes. Did the place sound empty — footsteps echoing, that sort of thing?"

"Yes, it did. I could hear them from quite a way off and I think the floor was concrete."

"Sounds like an old factory or workshop."

"Yes, it could have been." Chris struggled excitedly from Don's hold. "There was a church not far away because I heard the bell, so that must have been Sunday and there was a striking clock. The ringers weren't as good as ours."

"You've been there all the time? They never moved you?"

"Yes."

"Did you see them?"

"Not properly. They wore those funny masks, you know the sort you get from joke shops, but one slipped on the young one and I saw his chin. One had greyish sort of hair and the other's was fair, wavy and quite long."

"Did you ever see anyone else?"

"No."

"No sign of another prisoner?"

Jennifer caught her breath before his answer.

"No, but there might have been. It seemed quite a big place."

"Now think, Chris, have you any idea which way they went?"

"Oh, yes." He pointed unerringly in the opposite direction. "They went up the road and turned left."

"How — "

"Well, I'm sure they did because they didn't wait like you do when you go right but swerved straight off. Anyway, they slowed and waited for a car to pass before they turned right when they brought me. I heard them turn to go off."

"Half an hour — that way? Chris, if we drove back could you remember the turns?"

"I'll try."

"Don, surely the police should try this — Chris is tired, upset — "

"It takes time, Jenny. I won't subject Chris to anything unpleasant. If we could find the place — " he broke off and looked at her meaningly. "It could be very important."

"You mean Sue — "

"Yes, I won't drive about for long, then we'll take him straight home but the longer he waits the less likely he is to remember."

"Please, let's try to find them." Once over his ordeal Chris's natural resistance had reasserted itself and he was eager for the adventure.

"Jenny, come and sit with Chris at the back and I'll go slowly. Listen to the sounds of the road, Chris. The tyres make different noises according to what repair shape it's in. I can tell if we've gone off their road by that."

"They might not have gone back to the hide-out, Don," Jennifer reminded him and she got into the back with

Chris. Don fastened the driver's seat belt.

"It's a long shot. We know that but people are often careless when handling children. They underestimate their abilities. I think it's like this with Chris. It's worth a try."

They turned left at the corner and drove along the top road for about four minutes. Chris leaned forward listening intently.

"We came quite a long way along this road then we bumped over something — "

"A level crossing?"

"Yes, yes, it might have been."

"Good, that's a lead. If we don't hit one we know we're on the wrong road."

Jennifer said quickly, "I've got some chocolate in my bag Chris. Like some?"

He waved it away impatiently. "Not while I'm concentrating, thank you. I'm not hungry. They fed me quite well."

"Did they hurt you?"

"No, I got a bit bruised when I tried to dodge by the young one, one morning. He grabbed me and threw me about a bit, but they were all right really, only they didn't talk much and I got so bored all that time on my own." He turned an anxious gaze on her in the gloom of the car. "My grandmother? She's all right?"

"Yes, worried sick about you, of course."

"Poor Gran." He was contrite that in the excitement of the moment his first thoughts had not been for her. "That's it." He leaned forward again as the dim outline of the signal box, and the bump over the lines showed them they'd encountered the level crossing and were definitely on the right road.

"Now where, Chris? On a bit further?" Don picked up speed and Jennifer knew he was trying to establish the time context of the journey Chris had made earlier, though, of course, it was impossible to estimate the speed of the van.

"Yes, only a little way, then they turned and — " Chris shook his head, "I don't know after that. When we started we made several halts and turns and we wriggled quite a lot. I don't know."

Don slowed and peered at the signpost. "Two villages that way, straight on the next is five miles. Chris heard a church so we'll try right."

The first village was obviously not the one. It was reached by the road and seemed to consist of merely a straggle of houses on either side of it. No turns or bends had been made to reach it and though there was a church Don could see no building near-by which could possibly be the one young Chris had described. He turned the car.

"There was a turning further back to Rantby. I'll try that."

Chris was trembling either with cold or excitement Jennifer could not tell which. She doubted the wisdom of investigating this matter off their own bat. She now placed implicit trust in Don. Concerned though she was her whole heart sang a paeon of joy. Whatever reason kept Don in Stretton under a false name had nothing to do with the disappearance of either the child or Sue. Earlier tonight she'd known that by his concern for Pete Lawson, that sense of responsibility which told her he would never knowingly place another in jeopardy. She could dispel all her stupid fears. She loved Don and he was deserving of her faith in him.

Chris leaned forward and tapped Don's shoulder. "This feels like the right road. We wriggled round bends, like that last one, and there were houses. I heard dogs barking and we drew onto some gravel, that first evening when they took me. Did Grandmother pay them anything? Is that why they let me go? I jolly well hope she didn't." He exploded indignantly.

Don laughed. "I think there was an

attempt to place the ransom, but it wasn't picked up. That may be the reason they've got scared and dumped you. It's on the cards that even if we find the hide-out, the birds will have flown. Clearly they made plans to do so. We're coming into the village now. There's a church and a church clock. We might be quite close, so keep quiet now, Chris."

The village was deserted no chinks of light showing from any of the houses on both sides of the road. Jennifer held her wrist watch up to the car interior light. It was nearly five and twenty past midnight. Don drew the car up as quietly as he could close into the bend, near the church.

"Stay here you two. I'm going to reconnoitre round the back. There's an alley between the church and the pub."

"Don, surely this is much too close to the hub of the village. I'm sure people would have seen if — "

"Not necessarily if there's a private

back way to the workshop. The safest place to hide is among people."

They'd both been whispering and Chris's voice sounded over-loud in the silent street.

"Let me come. I can — "

"No," Don hissed. "You are to stay out of the way with Jenny."

"I never have any fun. I even missed the pageant." Jennifer caught back a laugh at his comically pathetic tone.

"I think you've had enough 'fun' as you call it to last a life-time and you haven't missed the pageant. I'm producing and I'll give you a part, probably as a page or herald." Don bent close to speak to them warningly. "As a matter of fact we may need you to play one of the princes so it's imperative that you and Jenny stay safe. You've both got important parts to play."

Jennifer forbore to mention that he was putting himself into the gravest danger of all, and he had the pageant's key role.

She kept a tight hold on Chris's arm as Don got out of the car and closed the door very quietly.

"I'll not be more than ten minutes. If we've drawn a blank we'll drive straight home."

Chris and Jennifer huddled together in the darkness of the back seat for Don had turned off all his lights. The boy had the sense to keep silent. Jennifer's thoughts raced to the likelihood of Chris's abductors now holding Sue Greenacre — but if so, why release Chris? It made no sense.

She jumped as a dark figure loomed up suddenly on the near side and she wound down the back window at Don's urgent whisper.

"The van's still there."

"What?"

"Round the back. There's a hut, probably an old scout hut, long disused, the grass is a mile high, there's a stream between the church-yard and the property behind — a square brick building. It might even have been an old chapel. There's an overgrown gravel drive, like the boy says, and a small green van."

"No lights anywhere?"

"Nothing I can see from this side. The place is secluded from the village by a screen of hawthorn. It's possible."

"They might have driven off in another car."

"True, but they might not. Look, Jenny, I want you to drive back to the cross-roads and make an emergency call. Inform the police you've got Chris safe then take him home to his grandmother. I'd rather you didn't use this phone over the road. You could alert somebody in the cottage and we don't want anybody rousing. Tell the police I'll wait for them in the church porch. They'll have the sense not to come on in with sirens sounding. Hurry, love."

"Don I can't leave you here."

He chuckled. "Why ever not, I'm not afraid of the bodies in the churchyard."

"But if they come out — see you — "

"They won't. I'm not going to advertise my presence."

"Why don't you come with me and let the police handle this? We can give directions."

"Jenny, I want to be here in case anybody leaves." His tone was grim and for a heart-stopping second she saw his danger.

"But what could you do? Don, you wouldn't tackle them?"

"The boy says there are only two. I'd certainly rouse the village, make some sort of fuss."

"Oh, Don," it was almost a wail, "let me ring the police and come back — "

"No, Jenny. You and the boy must get out of here. You said yourself he must be taken home now — as soon as possible. Don't worry, I'm not made of glass, you know. The chances are the worst danger I'm in is of catching cold in that chilly porch — waiting."

"If you catch them there'll be an identity parade, won't there?" Chris breathed ecstatically. Already he saw himself as the centre of attention. Clearly his unfortunate experience had left him none the worse. In a few days he would have forgotten his fears and bask in the glory of hero worship from the other children.

Jennifer climbed out and got into the driver's seat. "All right, but for heaven's sake, take care. You'd better have your anorak. Chris can take mine. I can put the car heater on."

The last sight of him she had was making for the church's side porch, his hands thrust deep into his anorak pockets.

12

JENNIFER thought she might have problems convincing the police that she was serious but to her relief, she was put through to the C.I.D. Department which was still concentrating on the Prevot kidnapping. A young detective listened to her without interruptions.

"Go to Mrs. Prevot with the child now, Miss Mitchell. Sergeant Hadley has given instructions to us to get in touch if any news comes in. I'll ring him at once. Don't worry about Mr. Wilson at Rantby. We'll go over immediately and with caution, naturally. I'll send a W.P.C. to you at Stretton to be with Mrs. Prevot and interview young Chris after he's rested."

Jennifer hung up and returned to the car. Chris was half out of the window listening for her.

"It will be all right. They'll ring your grandmother. We must get home now."

The Prevot house was ablaze with lights when she pulled up in the drive. Nance threw open the door almost before she had time to knock and Mrs. Prevot emerged immediately from the sitting-room in her dressing-gown, her eyes bright with tears and her arms wide. Chris flew straight into them and she held him close, both of them laughing and crying together in the joy of reunion.

Nance prepared sandwiches and coffee and Chris tucked into them appreciatively. When a second knock came Nance admitted a young attractive W.P.C. who introduced herself as Woman Constable Wright. Chris greeted her with enthusiasm and told her his story between gulps of coffee and comments on how good the sandwiches were.

"They might find — " Mrs. Prevot hesitated, looking hurriedly at Chris.

"We must hope — "

"I'm sure that was why Don took the step of retracing Chris's explanation of the way at once," Jennifer explained to W.P.C. Wright. "I know it seemed the wrong thing to do. We should have brought Chris home immediately but he was able to remember pretty clearly and we thought — "

"The time lag was so slight I think nothing but good could come from this," she said quietly. "Can I use your phone? I'll relay everything Chris has said back to headquarters. There might be some further hint."

Mrs. Prevot insisted on Jennifer eating while W.P.C. Wright was in the hall.

"Please, Miss Mitchell, some coffee at least." She made no suggestion that Jennifer should return to Ann's cottage. She appeared to have shrewdly assessed the situation and gauged the depths of Jennifer's terrible anxiety for Don. To please her, Jennifer sipped at coffee and nibbled a ham sandwich. Chris stoutly refused to go to bed and, wisely, no-one made him. It was obvious he wouldn't sleep until the affair was cleared up but as a couple of hours ticked by he lay cuddled against his grandmother on the settee and, despite his wild excitement, his eyes closed and he slept.

Jennifer was concerned lest the stress of the moment would affect Mrs. Prevot and whispered to Nance that it might be an idea to call Ann. The housekeeper agreed and Ann appeared within a quarter of an hour and administered a sedative which the old lady took without argument.

Ann drew Jennifer into the kitchen. "I called the doctor but he's out as usual. He gave me instructions about her, so she should be O.K. His wife promised to let him know and he'll come on, later. I think he ought to have a look at Chris, though, truth to tell, he seems all right."

Jennifer gave her a report on Pete and Ann sighed with relief. "Ted did ring me earlier, but I'm glad you spoke to him. The concussion doesn't appear serious." She glanced hurriedly at Jennifer, "He'll be safe, I'm sure. You're sick with worry."

"Don thinks there's just a chance that they're still holding Sue. He'll dash in, police or no police, if he thinks there's need. Ann, these men will be desperate. Things have gone wrong for them and — "

Ann reached over and took her hands, squeezing them hard. "Don't see dangers which don't exist, Jen. Don is nobody's fool. He won't risk anything in case he endangers Sue."

This was a comforting thought and Jennifer conceded it.

It was half past four before a car swished to a halt in the drive. Ann and Jennifer dashed into the hall with Nance as she opened the door. Sergeant Hadley raised one hand cheerily and Jennifer stood transfixed at sight of Don, tears of relief streaming down her cheeks. He stepped by the sergeant and took her into his arms.

"I'm O.K. Jenny, not a scratch. I didn't even do battle."

"Thank God. Oh Don, you idiot, I've been half out of my mind. Did you get them?"

"We did, Miss," Sergeant Hadley said, his tone expressing intense satisfaction. "Thanks to Mr. Wilson here."

Don drew Jennifer into the sitting-room, Chris hurled himself across the room.

"Yes, we got them."

"It was like I said, one fair and — "

"Yes, exactly as you said. They'd gone back to clear up all traces of your having been there. I suspected that they might that's why I insisted on taking Chris back along the road."

"Sue — ?"

"No trace. The two protested their innocence of any implication in her disappearance. They sounded so puzzled I think even Hadley was forced to believe them."

"I'm inclined to think this was their

first attempt. We don't know yet if they've records," the sergeant smiled at Chris's flushed face. "You seem to be all right, young man, that's a point in their favour. They'll go down for a long time, I imagine. High court judges and juries don't take to men who kidnap children and terrify old ladies."

"Then you are no further with your enquiries for Miss Greenacre, Sergeant?" Mrs. Prevot asked.

"No, we're still treating her disappearance seriously but she may, of course, have taken herself off."

He glanced briefly over W.P.C. Wright's notes; questioned Chris on one or two points and then rose to go.

"We'll leave you in peace now, Mrs. Prevot. Try not to concern yourself about proceedings. Everything will be made relatively easy for you and young Chris. You must be proud of him, he's a bright lad."

At the door he shook hands with Don. "Thanks, Wilson. I'll try to get to this pageant of yours." He grinned back at them. "I've always had an interest in the mystery of those princes in the Tower. I guess most policemen have."

Ann was clearly anxious that they should all leave and allow Mrs. Prevot to rest. Nature was asserting herself at last and Chris looked suddenly drawn and tired.

"Now remember, you do what the doctor says," Don told him. "I shall want you fresh for rehearsal on Friday." His lips twitched, "I think you're likely to be a quick learner."

Ann's car was in the drive and it took only two minutes to Ted's cottage. Don climbed out and, bending, kissed Jennifer hard, regardless of what Ann might think.

"That will hold me till tomorrow. There are things I have to say to you. For now, sleep tight, my Jenny."

Later, as she prepared to climb the stairs, Ann said dryly, "Still mistrust his motives?"

Jennifer shook her head. "No. He's promised to talk. He'll explain."

"I never knew a man yet who couldn't make a damn good try at it."

Jennifer blinked at her enquiringly.

"Go on, off you go. Keep the stars in your eyes. Nothing anybody says is going to make the slightest difference. You're head over heels in love with him, my girl. Trite as the expression is, the damage is done."

Achingly tired, Jennifer lay at last in the comfort of her bed. She went over and over again in her mind the clear picture of Don coping with the emergency of Pete's accident, then risking himself to assist the police in their search for Sue Greenacre. Whatever his reasons for deception, they could not matter — not now, and with that satisfying thought she slipped off into sleep.

13

THEY were both up late and, fortunately, Ann had no urgent calls, so they could take their time over breakfast. Jennifer went into the kitchen, calling back to Ann, over her shoulder.

"Boiled eggs do? I don't think I could fancy anything fried."

There was no answer so she went back into the sitting-cum-dining-room which did duty for both occasions. Ann was deaf to all her questions, intent on a letter.

"Oh, the post came then, Ann? What is it? Not bad news?"

"On the contrary, the best," Ann said quietly, handing over the page. "It's from Sue. Read it."

"Sue? You mean she's safe and writing to you? But why — "

"It explains. Read it. I'll finish getting

breakfast. We'll have it in the kitchen this morning."

"What? Oh, yes, of course."

A knot tightening in her stomach Jennifer stared at the pale green foreign-looking letter paper. The scrawled words swam before her eyes. She had been so anxious about Sue Greenacre — and guilt-ridden. She'd even doubted Don because of the girl's disappearance and his apparent lack of concern regarding it. Now Sue was calmly writing to Ann as if she were on holiday.

"I do hope I haven't caused too much trouble for the village. I know Daddy will never believe it but I can't go on letting him rule my life. I'm past sixteen so he couldn't force me back home but I know if I see him he'll over ride me. He always does.

"You remember I told you about Kurt. We really love one another. I suddenly had word from Kurt. I told him not to write because Dad makes such a fuss when I get letters from him. That last evening he rang me that he was waiting for me at a hotel in Leicester. It was so wonderful to hear his voice again. I didn't think about anything. I walked to the main road and got a bus.

"We've decided to get married. I can, with or without Dad's consent, now I'm here, but I think he'll come round in the end. He must or we'll lose everything, our happy memories, our love. I'm sure he'll realise all that's too precious to destroy by making a fuss with the authorities.

"It seemed utterly mad to go with Kurt with just the things I stood up in. I can only say that everything but my love for him was blotted out when he held me in his arms.

'Dear Ann, do be happy for me.
'I'm sorry about the pageant. Jennifer was so good at the last rehearsal, in spite of what that odious Mr. Wilson said, that I'm sure she will play the queen's part splendidly

and I know she can ride well.

'More the moment I'm settled. My love to everyone.

'Sue.'

There was no address. Obviously the writer was still anxious to play safe until she was sure of a reconciliation between herself and her father.

Ann had poured out Jennifer's coffee when she went into the kitchen.

"So Don was right."

Ann nodded. "It would appear so. I'm going past the Hall this morning. I'll call in on Sir Hugh, though I imagine she has also written to him. I think we ought to leave it to him to contact the police."

"I'll let Ted know when I'm in the branch."

The school was empty when she got there just before ten so she slipped next door to Ted's cottage. Don let her in.

"I'm looking for Ted," she said, a little breathlessly.

"He's taken the children up to the field for a final rehearsal. I want everything to go without a hitch tonight so he thought he'd iron out one or two problems. Have a coffee?"

"Thanks no. We were late having breakfast."

"Yes," he grinned. "We've all had a rough night. I'm off in a few minutes. I've promised to drive Mrs. Prevot and Chris into Leicester to the main police station. They want us all to make statements. Incidentally, Kevin's mother just phoned Ted. It *is* chicken-pox so I'll run through Prince Richard's part with young Chris this afternoon. He's a bright lad. I think he'll manage it for tomorrow, all right."

"But will he be fit? Are *you* really O.K. Don? I mean, did those two give any trouble and were you covering up last night to prevent Mrs. Prevot and me worrying?"

"So you really were worried about me, eh?" He drained his coffee cup. "I like that. It's a good sign."

She flushed scarlet.

"It's natural for me to worry. If it had been anyone else — "

"Don't spoil it, my Jenny. I have real hopes."

"Have you?" Her words were whispered. "Well, did you have trouble?"

"Much as it grieves me to disappoint you in your desire to see me as the true chivalrous hero, no. The police surrounded the place, shouted to them to come out through a megaphone and after an uneasy wait they did."

"Were they armed?"

"They'd left their weapons inside and came out with their hands up, but the police found plastic explosive, two revolvers and a shot gun."

"Explosives?"

"Frightening isn't it?" His tone was dry. "I think we were extremely fortunate that they decided to dump young Chris. The police made a thorough search. Though the two denied any knowledge of the whereabouts of Sue Greenacre I think Sergeant Hadley still hopes — "

"That's what I came to tell Ted about. She's safe. We've had a letter or rather Ann has. She ran away with a ski instructor she'd met at finishing school. They intend to marry. I gather there were quite a lot of objections from Sir Hugh. You appear to have summed her up well."

"Oh, I wasn't sure, but I've met the type." He raised a deprecating hand as Jennifer's head shot up. "Purely an observation from an experienced onlooker. Again, I like the reaction. Jealousy is the second excellent sign."

"Don — "

"Jenny, I told you. I've got a lot to say to you — and ask you, but not this moment. There are things to get straight first. You *do* trust me?"

He stood up and came to where she sat on the chintz-covered settee. Bending, he took both her hands in his, "Please, Jenny, have faith."

"I do, Don, truly."

"Then that's all that matters." He kissed her but it was devoid of passion.

She felt he was holding himself under a tight restraint. Her mind was still troubled. It was clear that she could no longer suspect Don of any criminal involvement but there were reasons why he could not yet declare himself. She could only guess at them. Was he married? Surely, if this were the case, he would have told her. In honour he felt that as yet he could not ask her to be his wife therefore there must be some other woman to whom he owed explanations? No, probably more than that.

A cold fear went through her. She loved him and yet could not be sure he was really hers. She did not doubt that he loved her — but she thrust away the warning that told her she had loved again and might even now, lose again.

He was watching her, and she knew he had not failed to note her agony of indecision. His own frown was troubled, then suddenly, he had assumed once more the attitude of light-hearted banter.

"Come on, my girl. There's work to do. The vicar's gone to pick up Pete. When you've finished at the mobile go over and see he's all right will you, then ring me at the police station. I may be there some time."

She spent the morning clearing up the branch work. Harry Lambert would come over tomorrow, of course, to see the pageant and she wanted to be sure the backlog of work was behind her. There would be a full-dress rehearsal tonight and tomorrow's first performance would take all her attention. They were to do six more over the next two weeks so it was imperative that she should be relatively free.

The phone was ringing insistently in Ted's cottage as she carried the last pile of books to the van. She stood for a moment uncertainly, then, knowing that Ted usually left his door unlocked, she went inside. The phone was still shrilling urgently so she picked up the receiver.

"Hello, can I speak to Mr. Lander please? It's important." The woman's voice sounded impatient and dominating.

"I'm sorry I think you must have the wrong number; this is Market Bosworth 3423."

There was a slight pause.

"Stowe's cottage?"

"That's right but there's no Mr. Lander living here."

"Mr. Stowe is the headmaster of the local school?"

"The Primary School, yes."

"I understood Mr. Lander was staying with Mr. Stowe at present."

The receiver jerked against Jennifer's ear and she almost stumbled, catching firm hold on the telephone table for support.

"I think you must be mistaken. Mr. Stowe has his nephew with him, Mr. Don Wilson."

"Oh," The listener's tone sharpened and she hesitated for a further moment.

"If you would leave your number I'll tell Mr. Stowe to call you back. He's expected in the schoolhouse at lunch time."

"And Mr. Wilson is out?"

"Yes. he is." Jennifer was cautious and did not reveal Don's destination.

"I'm sorry I troubled you. I must have been misinformed. Please don't bother Mr. Stowe."

Before Jennifer could ask anything further she was cut off. She replaced her receiver slowly.

It seemed she had discovered Don's name at last, Lander? But where was Don Wilson and who was the woman who demanded information in so proprietary a fashion?

14

THE dress rehearsal went tolerably well. In all events the villagers comforted themselves for its shortcomings by pointing out that it would be all right on the night itself.

Jennifer was miserably conscious that during the few opportunities which allowed him time to be with her, Don seemed unaware of her unhappiness. She made a poor showing of their scenes together, forgetting some of her lines and, on one occasion, an entrance cue. Ann looked at her anxiously.

"You feeling all right, Jen? Not sickening for something, are you?"

"Of course not, just tired, I expect, after the 'alarums and excursions' of last night."

"Has Don said something to upset you?"

"Nothing."

How could she explain that it was what Don failed to say, which troubled her.

Pete Lawson was cheered lustily as he rode onto the field and he gave a faultless performance, Rob Weston keeping firm control over the youngsters under his command.

The other 'star' of the evening was young Christopher whose costume fitted reasonably well and who gave a fair showing as the younger of the princes.

Ann reported that Sir Hugh had appeared more relieved than angry.

"Do you think he half suspected it?" Jennifer asked her.

"Well, I gather they've had harsh words over Kurt Spengler. I think he'll do what Sue says in the letter, accept the situation as it is, if he doesn't, he'll lose Sue."

"Altogether he'd become a very lonely old man in that event."

Ann was hooking herself into Jennifer's former costume as Jane Shore.

"I've arranged for a locum nurse to be on call here tomorrow," she said, thoughtfully regarding herself in the mirror. "Barring a full-scale emergency I should manage for the big performance. Next week," she shrugged expressively, "we can but hope."

They were running late and Don had decided to run through the battle scenes first on the field and to keep some of the later theatre scenes for try-out in the schoolroom.

"We're bound to be going on after dark," he said. "There's so many loose ends to tie up and it doesn't matter for us once the children are sent off to bed."

It had looked like rain earlier and the younger members of the cast were concerned for the show tomorrow. Old Josh Harris had laughed at their fears.

"No sign of rain yet. Oi knows what oi'm talking about. T'will be fair tomorrow, you mark my words."

Certainly it was now warm in the brocaded costume with its heavy fur trimming. Jennifer remarked on it to Ann then caught her breath as she saw her friend properly for the first time.

Ann looked superb in the scarlet gown with its gold braid and embroidery. The tall headdress gave her added height, off-setting her plumpness and Ann's dark mischievous air was perfect for the portrayal of the King's merry mistress.

"Ann, that's quite breathtakingly beautiful on you," she said, as she adjusted the yards of veiling on the nurse's cloth of gold hennin.

"You can say that again."

They both turned hastily from the long pier glass as Pete Lawson emerged from his dressing-room where he had discarded his armour. He could not take his eyes from Ann who dowered her gaze hastily, gathered up her voluminous skirts and prepared to move towards the schoolroom.

"Wait, Ann." Pete held out an arm to detain her. "You really do look wonderful. I'm — that is, we're delighted you can play a bigger part after all. It's a shame the way you keep having to dash off all the time. You miss a lot of fun."

"Well I'm glad you're well enough to play your part, Peter."

"Oh, it wasn't serious, but I'm going to make damned sure I hold the brute in well tomorrow."

She smiled and nodded. Others were coming from the dressing-room now, anxious to view themselves in the long mirror.

He bent towards her. "After the show tomorrow-night, dinner at the Country Club? Just the two of us."

Ann's pretty face flushed rosily. "Why, Pete — I — yes, I'd love that but won't you want to be with your friends? I mean — "

"Not tomorrow night, I won't," he said hurriedly. "Oh, sorry, Jennifer, am I keeping you both?"

"That's O.K., Pete. Are you ready now, Ann?"

"Yes." Ann looked back at him

smiling, "I'll look forward to it, Peter. It's sweet of you to invite me."

"It's a good job I saw you first," he grinned. "Once they see you in that gown they'll be queuing up."

Ann looked hastily down at the low frontage and Jennifer caught her hand laughing.

"That's not what Pete meant," she assured her. "The whole outfit is very becoming."

They were forced to sit for a moment waiting for their cues and Jennifer found herself watching her friend's reactions to the rehearsal. Not once did she take her eyes from Pete Lawson. When she caught Jennifer's gaze she fidgeted nervously with some imitation jewels on the gilded belt at her waist.

Jennifer said quietly, "I hope things go well for you, Ann. Pete's such a grand chap."

Ann nodded ruefully. "He is that. I've always — liked him." There was a slight hesitation before the verb and she laughed up at Jennifer. "Well, you've guessed it, my secret longing. He's never taken the slightest notice of me before. It must be this glamorous gown. Of course, before, there was always Sue around."

Jennifer had noted before that one odd note of envy when they'd been talking about Sue Greenacre. So Pete had been smitten.

Ann continued. "I don't think there was ever anything serious but she just ran around with the youthful crowd. I've never had much opportunity. I could never promise to go anywhere or do anything in case I was called out."

"You must have been frantic the other night. You never said a word about it."

"Well, I wasn't on the spot so could only guess at what might be wrong. Anyway, in my position, you try not to panic. We had problems of our own that night with Mrs. Prevot and Chris." She sighed happily. "Everything's cleared up now, Chris is safe and Sue. We can enjoy the pageant without doubts hovering over us all the time."

Jennifer wished she could agree with her. She looked to where Don was in close consultation with Ted and the other of tomorrow's 'commanders'. As if aware of her scrutiny he glanced up at her and smiled. She hoped her answering one did not appear as forced as it felt.

"Right, Jenny, let's run over our scene together again, shall we?"

She climbed unwillingly to her feet. She'd made such a mess of it previously and she really must not let him down. If only she could put aside her doubts about the unknown Mr. Lander.

He took her chilled fingers and led her onto the cleared space which did duty as an improvised stage.

"You all right, Jenny? Your hands are icy."

"Stage fright before the event, I wouldn't wonder," she said hastily. "It all seems so close now and frightening."

"Follow my leads and you can't go wrong."

She looked into those cool grey — green eyes of his and wondered. Had the real Anne Neville had doubts about her Richard? Did she harbour the terrifying thought that he'd really been responsible for the deaths of those two helpless princes in the Tower of London? Don was eyeing her questioningly and she mentally gave herself a shake, consigned her problems to the back of her mind and concentrated hard on the rehearsal.

Afterwards he drew her aside as they hungrily bit into sandwiches and cakes provided by Mary Norton and her helpers.

"That was fine. You've really nothing to worry about. Try and get a good night's sleep. You're still trembling."

"Sleep, he says. I'll never manage a wink. I shall be going over and over my lines. Aren't you worried Don? Suppose we make a mess of the whole thing with the Press and

213

Council Bigwigs all there — ?"

He shrugged. "I'm not supposing it will go wrong, not badly at any rate. They'll be places of course, where it could be better. There always are, even in professional performances. I'm as satisfied as I could ever hope to be."

She said softly, "Aren't you having friends down tomorrow?"

"My parents are hoping to make it, yes, and a couple of close friends from London, Bill, bless him, will want his car back."

Her heart thudded uncomfortably. Was the other 'friend' a woman, the one who'd phoned him earlier? Should she mention it?

"You haven't talked about your parents."

"No, I haven't, have I? I see them so rarely. That's not because we fail to get on. I adore them both. Dad's retired now, of course, but he'll be critical of the performance," he added dryly and she forced a smile. "Mum

214

thinks everything I do is wonderful, naturally."

Jennifer was about to ask if either was brother or sister to Ted but bit it back. That might force Don to lie further and it would prove nothing.

"What did your father do?"

"He was a chartered accountant. He's never quite forgiven me for not joining the firm. I've arranged for the four of us to have dinner together."

"But Don — "

"At the Red Lion in Bosworth. It seems everyone is making for the Country Club and I shall want some privacy." He bent and stroked her fingers down the slender bones of her hand. "You don't have to worry about the meeting, Jenny, I assure you."

"There's someone I want you to meet."

"I understood your parents were dead."

"They are. These are Ken's people. I love them very much."

He looked full at her and nodded

215

gravely, "I understand. I'll look forward to meeting them."

When Don was putting some of the men through their final paces Cliff came to Jennifer's side.

"Is everything all right with you, Jennifer?"

"Yes, Cliff, I think so."

He hesitated. "I've seen you together, thought that that everything was settled, but tonight, you seem very unsure of yourself."

"Do I? I'm sure I had no idea I gave that impression."

"You *do* love him?"

"Yes, I do."

"He's asked you?"

"To marry him? No, not yet."

"But — "

"I think there are problems." She kept her voice low and turned her head away. Cliff was so observant. He would read in her eyes her doubts and fears.

"You think he may not be free. Damn him, Jennifer. Why?"

216

"Cliff, I didn't say that. I don't know."

"I could sort him out."

She caught back a half hysterical laugh. "No, Cliff. You will not say one word to Don. Promise."

"I've always been very fond of you, Jen. I won't have him ill-use you."

"Cliff, you mustn't make a scene. Don has not proposed. I believe he loves me as I do him, but I have no right to assume as much, so please, no confrontations. I know how anxious you are to help, but it wouldn't do, not at all."

He squeezed her hands tightly. "All right, Jen, if you say so, but you know you can rely on me."

"Thank you I know it and bless you, my dear."

Her eyes were misted with tears and she shook them angrily away when Pete and Ann came towards her laughing. God willing, these two would find real happiness. They deserved each other.

15

THE opening fanfare of trumpets made Jennifer jump as she applied the finishing touches to her make-up. As old Josh had promised it was a fine day and people had been pouring into the spectator stands for over an hour.

Ken's parents had come to the cottage with Harry to see her before the performance.

"You look a little drawn, Jennifer," Mrs. Sutton said quietly when she had a chance to speak with her alone. "Has the strain been a little too much for you?"

"Not really. It was, at first, but the villagers have been so friendly."

"Any particular friends?" Mary's kindly face expressed feminine curiosity and Jennifer laughed, trying hard not to blush too obviously. She'd mentioned

Cliff and Don in her letters to the Suttons. Had Mary read between the lines?

"Yes," she admitted, "one I'm specially anxious for you to meet." She looked up suddenly. "You won't mind — too much?"

"My dear, I told you, we shall only mind if you go on being so dreadfully unhappy. Is he right for you, Jennifer? You look," she searched for the right word, "uncertain, somehow."

"There are difficulties. Oh, Mary, I wish I could explain but I wouldn't know where to begin, anyway there's no time. I'll come down and see you tomorrow, if I may."

"Good. We'll have a long talk."

Harry had hurried them away to their reserved places while Jennifer went to the dressing-cubicles. Don was waiting near the entrance. He'd changed and was waiting to adjust his jewelled chain before the communal mirror.

"You're a bit late. I was beginning to get worried about you."

"You didn't think I'd let you down."

"I knew you'd never do that if you could help it."

Cliff came out of his cubicle and nodded at them. There was still a reserve between him and Don though they did not argue any more. Cliff looked resplendent in scarlet and cloth of gold.

"Some of the Society crowd came round asking for you, Jen. They've had to go in, now, of course."

"I'll look for them afterwards, thank you, Cliff. Good luck."

"Thanks and the very best of luck to both of you."

He went out across the grass to take his place in the wings and now the others had moved off and they were alone. Don put his hands on her shoulders and tilted up her chin. In his eyes she read how much the success of the performance meant to him and her own eyes widened in surprise.

"It will go well, Don. I'm sure of it. You've worked so hard. Everyone will do his and her best. Don't worry about Cliff. He's not mean-minded."

"I'm not worried about Cliff. He's a good loser, I believe. I'll admit to a rumbling in the stomach now it's on us, I want to bring it to a successful conclusion. It is necessary."

She kissed him full on the lips. "Take that for luck. I must hurry and change now. Go over to them. They'll all be nervous and they need you."

He nodded and, bending, kissed her hard in answer.

"See you."

She watched him until he was drawn into the little circle of waiting actors and then hurried inside to change. The Suttons and Harry had delayed her and she struggled with the unfamiliar hooks on her gown. Now the trumpets were reminding her that she would soon need to be in position ready for her cue.

At last she was ready and scrutinising her make-up critically.

A voice behind her made her jump

and turn, slightly alarmed.

"I'm sorry, did I startle you? I'm looking for Guy Lander. Is he here?"

The voice had a faintly American intonation and the newcomer was a woman in her late twenties or early thirties. She was attractive and smartly dressed in a strawberry-coloured suit of crushed velvet and what Jennifer was sure was a pure silk blouse. That excellent simplicity could only be Paris designed, and the shoulder bag and shoes were expensive too, leather. The best quality. Jennifer's quick glance took in dark hair, short but shiny and styled by an expert. Like her clothes the cut was simple and designed to complement her small oval-shaped face and fine dark eyes. She moved well too, not with Sue's unconscious youthful grace, but with the assurance of a woman who knew just what she wanted and always got it.

"Mr. Lander, can you tell me where he is?" She pressed her question gently but inexorably.

Jennifer's stiff lips found it difficult to frame her words.

"You must be mistaken, there's no-one by that name."

The woman smiled faintly then shrugged. "Your producer. It doesn't matter what you call him. He's smallish, dark, possibly a mite sullen." Her expression showed that she understood that Jennifer had recognised her description.

"I'm Clare Stainer. I'd like to see him before the performance — please."

The voice was lovely, a trace of huskiness overlaying the well modulated warmth of a trained performer. Jennifer was convinced that the woman was an actress, and a successful one, if her appearance was anything to go by.

"That would be difficult," she stammered. "He's very busy."

"My dear, I know only too well, that on the 'night' no-one is less needed than the producer. Everyone is thankful if he takes himself off to the nearest bar and stops hovering."

"Don — Mr. Lander, if that is the man you mean, is playing Richard the Third."

"He is? That *is* interesting." She considered. "Is he on right at the beginning?"

"Well, yes, then there are a couple of scenes without him, but — "

Clare Stainer looked down at Jennifer's costume.

"You are obviously playing a principal part. Don't let me detain you. If you could slip behind the stage and tell Don I'm here I'd be grateful."

"Couldn't it wait — your business, until after the performance?"

"It could, but I think he'd rather see me now."

"I'll see what I can do."

"Is there somewhere I can wait?"

"In here. I'll find you a stool."

"Thanks. Don't worry about me. I'll be O.K."

"I'm to tell him who you are?"

Clare Stainer smiled. She really was a beautiful woman even if her voice and manner were somewhat studied.

"You think he's been hiding from me, honey, using this other name. Don — what was it?"

"Wilson."

"Oh yes. There are — reasons. You needn't disturb yourself I'm not going to cause a scene." Her lovely lips twisted in a wry gesture. "It's not my way."

"No, of course not. I'm going over now. I must or I'll miss my cue. I'll tell Don you're here."

"You were the one who answered the phone yesterday."

"Yes I'm librarian here, Jennifer Mitchell."

"I'm delighted to see you, Miss Mitchell. I'm sure you'll do well. You look fabulous in that blue brocade, as if you'd stepped from one of those old manuscripts in the British Museum."

"Thank you." Jennifer felt herself breathless. She often did under stress. "I'll send someone back with refreshments for you. I could try and find

you a seat but we're fully booked
and — "

"Another time. It's just Guy I want
to see."

"Of course."

Jennifer gave her a nod and hurried
out of the cubicle. She stood uncertainly
outside the mobile hut and looked
unhappily towards the stage. Applause
burst through at the end of the scene,
spontaneous and delighted. She bit her
lip. Why should Clare Stainer insist on
seeing Don now? Was she his wife?

Whatever the problem it could surely
wait until afterwards. Jennifer had been
touched by the intensity of Don's desire
for success. At first the whole thing
had seemed a chore to him and rather
a boring one at that. Suddenly it
was imperative that the pageant went
well. His future career might very well
depend on it. Obviously he had no
desire to see Clare Stainer. If he had he
would have invited her and he wouldn't
be here masquerading as Ted Stowe's
nephew.

Whatever the rights and wrongs of it, Jennifer was determined that the performance should proceed as planned. Clare Stainer must not be allowed to interfere. She had promised not to cause a scene, but she might well do so and Don could be too upset to continue.

The key was in the outside lock. The cast were all out, back stage. On impulse Jennifer drew the door across. It went to without noise and determinedly she turned the key, then, running into the second hut, she hid it under one of the performer's make-up boxes. No-one would need to go back yet — if they did, they'd find it or the keys were probably all alike. For a time at least Clare Stainer would be prevented from making trouble.

"Jennifer?" Cliff's voice sounded urgent and troubled. "Ah, there you are. You're on in two minutes. Don's worried." He checked as she held her skirts high and ran down the steps to him. "Anything wrong?"

"No, of course not. Is it going well?"

"Splendidly." He beamed his enthusiasm. "Better than we could have hoped."

"Good. I hope I don't ruin it."

She breathed a heartfelt prayer, that she hadn't indeed caused further complications in Don's affairs.

16

JENNIFER stood with Cliff, Ann and some of the other performers as the final scenes of the pageant unfolded.

It was almost ended, that brief tragic reign that was to leave historians with the great question. Had Richard III, the last of the Plantagenet kings, murdered his young nephews, or did Henry Tudor, that brilliant statesman who was to emerge the victor of this battle, blacken his predecessor's name for political reasons or himself destroy the lives of the two young boys which stood between him and the succession?

The spectators had left their wooden stands and gone up to Ambien. The armies were in position and as Jennifer had dreamed that first afternoon she saw it from the bedroom window of

Ann's cottage, time itself had rolled back and that historic confrontation was now being enacted before their eyes.

The trumpets sounded and Pete Lawson as Norfolk led the van of the king's army down the ridge of the hill while Rob marched his men to engage them. No-one spoke. There was just the sound of horses' hoofs, the jingle of accoutrements. All eyes were focused on the blaze of heraldic colours, the royal standard with its leopards and lilies, Richard's personal device of the White Boar, the lion of Norfolk. A horse neighed, another snorted, then a ringing command and the men engaged with a thunderous clashing of weapons and yelling of battle cries.

Jennifer's eyes sought and found Don as the dying rays of the setting sun stained his armour blood-red. Proud and aloof he reined in his big white gelding on the brow of the hill.

Tears blinded her later as she watched that gallant final charge when defeat was close and the young king risked everything on a last attempt to find and kill his enemy, Henry Tudor, then there were the cries of 'Treason' as the king was traitorously attacked from the rear and he was unhorsed and hacked to his death.

The excitement which had beset the spectators quietened again as the body of the dead king, stripped of his armour, was slung across his big white war-horse, and led from the battlefield by the young herald. It was so moving that the hush continued for quite some moments afterwards, then gradually, people relaxed and all around her Jennifer heard the enthusiastic comments.

"Wonderful. I don't know when I've seen anything so colourful. Much better than a film."

"You really thought you were there — "

"Weren't the horses marvellous?"

"Well?" Cliff smiled at her. "Satisfied?"

"It did seem to go well. Did you

231

think so? Poor Don, I should think he must feel quite sick, Prince didn't like the chanting of those monks. When he reared I thought Don might be thrown."

"He thought that might happen, I gather, and had himself lashed in very securely."

Ann came hurrying up with Pete looking remarkably well after his 'death' some moments earlier.

"Isn't it thrilling?" Ann's eyes sparkled with delight. "Don and Ted are hemmed in by reporters and photographers. You're wanted, you two."

Don held out his hand to draw Jennifer close as she drew back.

"Thank you, gentlemen, I'm glad you all enjoyed the performance. Allow me to present my queen our librarian, Miss Jennifer Mitchell. Not only did she play the part splendidly but she also acted as our historical advisor and arranged the book display in the centre."

He beckoned Cliff into the group.

"Mr. Clifford Norris, assistant at the school, who played King Edward. He was also responsible for training our youthful men-at-arms and keeping them clear of danger. I don't know what I should have done without him."

Jennifer fought clear of her admirers to touch Don's arm.

"Thank you. It was good of you to give Cliff a commendation. It will go down well with the educational authorities."

"There was nothing insincere about what I said. Cliff is an excellent organiser. If he gets promotion, Ted will be heartbroken, though he'd never stand in his way. Well, Jenny, my love, we did it."

"Everyone seems pleased."

"Pleased, they are amazed." Ted pushed through the group to their side. "Don, your parents are waiting to congratulate you, but can you speak to this chap from *The Times?*"

"What? Yes, I suppose so."

A young man in a leather jacket

scribbled in his notebook.

"How many took part? No professionals, at all? You *do* surprise me. The timing had the earmarks of the very experienced professional producer. What did you say you did, sir?"

"I didn't," Don said a little curtly. "I have drama connections. I did this as a favour for a friend. When people are really enthusiastic they often do as well as paid actors. We mustn't be patronising."

"Some film producers are noted for preferring to engage ordinary bystanders and townspeople. That's so, isn't it? Guy Lander was particularly successful for that type of work."

The colour drained from Jennifer's cheeks as she saw by the little tic working in Don's temple that he was angry. Clearly the man had recognised him and was baiting him. Don looked beyond the reporter to an elderly couple whom Ted was assisting across the battlefield. His grip tightened on Jennifer's arm.

"Excuse me," he said brusquely and brushed by the press-man.

Don obviously resembled his mother. She was quite small and sturdy, though she'd not yet run to fat. His father was a tall, hatchet-faced man who had once probably been very distinguished looking.

Don halted Jenny in his sudden rush towards them so that she almost stumbled.

"This is Jenny," he announced.

"So I gathered."

Jennifer thought Don's mother did not grant friendship any more easily than her son did, but decided that once having won her approval it would be worth having. The older woman held out her hand in greeting.

"It would be a cliché to say that we've already heard a great deal about you, Jenny. I hope we shall be friends."

Jennifer was a little bemused. Don's mother had a pleasant but shrewd face and she wondered how much he had told her. Could she, Jennifer, address these people as Mr. and Mrs. Wilson?

She murmured some commonplace greeting, feeling rather foolish. Don's father's hand grip was firm but welcoming.

"You look very charming, my dear."

Her dilemma was cut short by the arrival of young Christopher Prevot on the scene. He'd been running hard, was extremely breathless and still wearing his costume as prince Richard.

"Don, please. Have you got the key to our dressing hut?"

Don looked mystified. "Key? I didn't know there was one. Why?"

"There's a lady locked in there. I was just going by and I heard her call out. I thought it was funny so I went up close. It doesn't sound like anybody I know. She said she'd been pushing at the door for ages. I tried to open it but it won't budge. She said she was sure it was locked from the outside."

"Did you tell Mr. Stowe?"

"He's in the Church Hall with the bigwigs, the Lord Lieutenant and — "

"Quite," Don said dryly. "We can hardly disturb him. I'd better come back with you."

He turned to his parents. "Sorry, I seem to be saying 'excuse me' all the time today but you know how things are. Jenny, could you go with them to the Church Hall? Introduce them to your friends."

Thankfully Jennifer saw Ann approaching and attracted her attention.

"I'd better go with you, Don. If it's one of the girls she might be undressed and — Ann, would you take Don's friends to Mr. Stowe at the visitor's table." She hastily introduced her friend. "This is Ann Trevor who shares her cottage with me."

"Of course, only too pleased to." Ann smiled at Don and shook hands with each of his parents. "I'm glad everything went so marvellously. Pete was great, wasn't he? My heart was in my mouth when his horse started down the slope. Aren't you two coming for coffee?"

"Not just for a moment," Don explained. "There's a bit of a flap on. Tell Ted I'll only be a few minutes."

Jennifer told herself it might have been wiser to leave Don and Claire Stainer to meet without her being present but she could not resist the overwhelming desire to observe this meeting, even if Claire Stainer made an ugly scene and accused her, publicly, of locking her in the dressing-room. At least, Jennifer thought, mutinously, the ruse worked. The performance was over and an unqualified success.

"Everybody's gone to the Church Hall," Chris explained as he scrambled to keep in step with Don's hasty strides, "so I couldn't get anyone to help. I wouldn't have gone there myself but Gran sent me back for a handkerchief. I was sniffing."

Don nodded curtly and they pulled up short near the dressing-hut. Jennifer was relieved to discover that Claire Stainer was not the type of woman to lose her dignity by screaming for assistance, though she had probably seen Chris from a window and decided to dispatch him for some help.

Don tried the door then moved to the far side where the windows were sited and peered in.

"You in there, I'm sorry. The door appears to have banged to and locked. I'll see if the key to the other hut fits. Fetch it, Chris. You could have tried that at first, you know."

"I never — "

"Thought. Yes, I know, but hurry."

Jennifer's heart beat uncomfortably while they waited. She felt like she had at school when she'd been summoned to the headmistress's study to face judgement for some stupid prank. Let's face it, she thought, I've behaved like some idiotic schoolgirl. Don will be furious. Claire made no answer from the inside and Chris returned triumphantly with the second key.

Don hurriedly inserted it in the lock and stood back. The door opened easily and Claire Stainer, as poised as ever, paused on the step.

"Well, thanks very much. I was beginning to feel really claustrophobic in there."

"Claire." Don made no attempt to avoid her openly acknowledging him. "What in hell are you doing in there?"

Claire Stainer looked beyond him to Jennifer.

"I went in to look for someone who could find you. As you said, the door probably banged to imprisoning me." Her raised eyebrow directed at Jennifer warned her to keep silent. "I'm sorry, Guy, but you've led me a hard dance. I rang yesterday and someone said you weren't here but your mother told me — "

"Oh, forget that." He pushed aside his masquerade as if it had never existed, went to her and kissed her soundly. "By heck, it's good to see you. You're looking great."

Jennifer's legs trembled under the stiff brocade folds of her costume. For the moment neither of them seemed to acknowledge her presence. They were so intent in their delight at the meeting.

"When did you arrive? Did you fly?"

A flicker of apprehension crossed Claire Stainer's features which Jennifer could not fail to notice.

"Yes, I had several business meetings. I had to, then I heard you were working on this production — " Claire recalled Don to the fact that they weren't alone. "Guy, I must have a word with you. Is it all over?"

"Yes."

"And it went well?"

"Very well."

Claire gave a little sigh. "Thank God."

Don turned to Chris. His expression begged Jennifer wordlessly not to demand explanations yet. He shrugged helplessly.

"Jenny, forgive me, I have to talk to Claire — unfinished business. Go with Chris, please. I'll be in in less than half an hour — please."

"Yes, of course."

Jennifer nodded coolly to Claire as Don briefly introduced them. "I understand. I must find Harry and the Suttons anyway."

She held her head high and tried to attend to Chris's chatter, as he drew her along the footpath to the Church Hall. She was close to breaking down, but she must mingle with the guests, accept congratulations, behave naturally, until she could get away somewhere to hide her grief from the world. Don was thrilled to see Claire and that woman's behaviour in magnanimously letting Jennifer off the hook told only too plainly, that she was very sure of Don.

17

AWAY from the chattering and bantering in the Church Hall it seemed very lonely on this quiet part of the battlefield. It was dusk and quite chilly. Jennifer wished she'd had the courage to return to the changing huts but she could not have faced Don and Claire Stainer. She'd sought privacy away from the crowd.

It had been maddening to have all her old friends in London push round her with their compliments. In their enthusiasm for the excellence of the performance, they'd forgotten their old embarrassment over the death of Ken Sutton. They'd all known Jennifer and Ken in the early days of their engagement. Now they were full of admiration for all the work that had been done at the Centre and they'd travelled down specially to see the pageant. At any other time Jennifer would have welcomed the opportunity to renew old friendships and she smiled and nodded at Cliff's side, laughed at the old teasing.

"What does it feel like to be Richard's wife, Jen?" one of them said. "How does Don himself view the character of Richard? His performance seemed a sympathetic one."

She answered mechanically. "Oh, he's taken a great deal of trouble to research carefully. He was a bit cutting at first, but I think we've converted him to our way of thinking."

Nicola, a friend of long standing, and a former workmate in London said, "Isn't he like the portraits? I caught my breath when he first stepped on the stage."

That time he'd ridden across the field he'd done the same to Jennifer. Had she fallen in love with him for the foolish romantic notion that he resembled the king she so admired?

She'd escaped at last after promising

the Suttons she'd drive over tomorrow and come here alone. It hadn't been easy to escape Cliff's vigilance. She'd feared he'd declare a wish to come with her and she had to be alone. There'd been no sign of Don or Claire Stainer. Had he driven her back to her hotel?

She reached out to touch the rough stone memorial which marked the spot where the king had died. Was she being sentimental? Had Don appeared at the psychological moment and because of the uncanny resemblance, she'd fallen madly for him?

She thought back over the last weeks and knew it wasn't so. She loved Don for himself even during the moments when she'd doubted him. That night he'd taken charge over Pete and put himself into danger to discover the hide-out of young Chris's kidnappers, her heart had gone out to him. Sullen and arrogant he could be, a hard taskmaster, but there was no meanness in him. Cliff Norris had made him look foolish but he'd ridden that out, not taken advantage of the situation to make trouble for Cliff or even spoil his chances of taking part. Just now he'd put in a good word for Cliff which would stand him in good stead in the future.

Yet what did she really know of him? His name was Lander, and he was a good actor and producer. What did he do? Where did he live? She had never even stopped to ask herself if she was ready to uproot herself and just go with him — anywhere he wished. It had seemed perfectly natural that she should be prepared to trust him, despite the prickles of warning that had been with her from the beginning.

Now it seemed she wouldn't have the chance. He'd welcomed Claire Stainer with open arms. She straightened her shoulders determinedly. He'd done one thing for her. She could face life again, even if she had to do without Don. Harry's plan had paid off. She must go back and change. It was becoming a little frightening here in the ghostly half light.

Then she saw him. He was hastening towards her and as she came close she saw he was frightened.

"Jenny, thank God. I looked everywhere else, then it occurred to me you might have come here. My dear girl, you'll catch your death. Why didn't you change into your trousers and put on a thick sweater?"

He was wearing a murrey velvet dinner jacket and had obviously meant to go to the Red Lion to join his parents. She'd forgotten them, in her misery.

"Where's Claire?" She deliberately made herself face the truth, unpleasant though it might be.

"Claire? She's gone back into Leicester."

"Who is she, Don, your wife? Girlfriend?"

He halted abruptly and his face cleared of its bewilderment.

"Neither. Claire is a very old friend, a good friend, one who has worked with me very closely in the past and whom I'll always be grateful to — for lots of things."

Jennifer gave a little sob, "Then why — "

"Why did I tell everyone in the village I was Don Wilson?" His tone softened and he came close, stripped off his jacket and put it round her shoulders. "It was a mad thing but I didn't think of the repercussions at the time. Come on, love, let's get back to the village."

"No, Don, I must know — now."

"All right. Come and perch here for a moment on this gate."

She was glad of his nearness, safe in his encircling arms. If Claire was nothing to him she could hope again.

"Don Wilson is my friend. We met at Drama School. He wanted to teach, I to produce. I did some television work, then I got a chance to go to the States." He paused and his voice became oddly muffled as he turned from her.

"That was when I met Claire Stainer and her sister Amanda."

"Mandy Stainer. Oh I remember now. I saw her in — but she was killed, some months ago."

"Yes, she was killed, working on my new film."

"Oh Don, why didn't I realise when Claire asked for you. You produced 'The King's Commander' that marvellous film about Rupert of the Rhine. Didn't it get an Academy award?"

"It did. It was my first big chance and it paid off handsomely. This new epic was an adventure film set in the early days of flying. Mandy had been my leading lady in 'The King's Commander' and we — we'd fallen in love, planned to marry, when Mandy's divorce came through. The delay seemed to spell disaster. Perhaps it was as well. I'd worked in television with Claire. I think in her own way

Claire tried to warn me off Mandy. She knew her only too well. At first it was breathtaking. We went to Europe. Our feet seemed not to touch the ground, then I began to realise how nervy she was. If the slightest thing went wrong even if she didn't get the meticulous attentions she thought she ought to have in hotels and restaurants, she'd get into the most appalling rages. It was terrifying. You'd think she'd have a heart attack or kill the offender. I had to swallow the embarrassment, then there were times I literally had to buy her out of legal scrapes, and of course, she drank too much."

"You went on loving her?"

"I told myself none of it would make any difference. When we were married she'd quieten down — there'd be children — but she soon made it clear that there'd be no life of that kind. We began to row incessantly and I knew we'd have to break it off before Mandy became so dependent on me that that wouldn't be possible."

His arm tightened on her shoulder and she knew he was living again the bad times, the moments of guilty indecision.

"I'd engaged a stunt man, Glen Charles. He was a brilliant flyer and about as wild as Mandy wanted to be; they saw each other a lot. Even when he wasn't needed he took to hanging around the set." Don swallowed, "The trouble is I shall blame myself till the day I die that I chose that particular day for our final and classic row. Glen had been seen out the night before with Mandy. I wouldn't have minded so much about that if she hadn't lied about it. It was the last straw. I wanted 'out' and took the opportunity to throw Glen Charles in her face. We screamed at each other in her dressing-room." He gave the little helpless shrug Jennifer knew so well, "I should think the whole of the studio staff could hear us. Mandy could be pretty crude when she chose and she *did* choose that morning. I was so disgusted that I hit her. She stood there with that great scarlet mark across her cheek, but oddly enough she seemed to calm down. I thought she'd break down and cry. She told me to 'Get out' and I did. There didn't seem much point in continuing shooting that day so I told the crew they could knock off. We'd planned to shoot the crash scene. Glen, naturally, was doing the flying and he'd worked out the simulation to the last detail. It should have been accident proof — only it wasn't."

Jennifer's hand stole up to touch his face. He was sweating. Even now he was actually experiencing the terrible events of that crucial work-day.

"About ten minutes later Mandy came out of the dressing-room and said she was ready to go on with the scene. I told her I'd dismissed the crew. She told me not to be such a damned fool. Actually she put it more forcibly than that. Time cost money in picture-making and we'd got a deadline to meet. I called back the camera man and crew. They didn't object and drove off to the location site and prepared the scene. God, I can remember now that I was so immersed in getting the shots right I put this whole damn scene right behind me. The story line called for Mandy to elope with the pilot, Glen Charles. He looked a bit sheepish in his leather flying coat with the fur collar, mooched about with his hands in his pocket. He'd got one of those pencil moustaches, it was the period fashion. Funny how everything about the day is etched in my mind razor sharp. Mandy was wearing a coat with a great fur collar as well. She looked so young and innocent. She was a lot like Claire only fairer, more ethereal looking, but you've seen her in movies — "

Jennifer swallowed and nodded.

"She climbed into the cockpit and we went through the whole routine of winding the propeller, making contact. Glen gave the thumbs up and they took away the chocks and he was airborne. Cameras whizzed. He flew low, he knew his stuff all right. We'd no problems, everything going well, no need for re-takes — till the plane plumeted. You've heard people use that trite old simile 'like a wounded bird'. Well, it was, exactly like that. We could only stand like idiots with our mouths open till it hit with a kind of dull thud, quieter than you'd believe and there was a second or two before it exploded then all hell was let loose."

Jennifer waited while he mastered himself. His voice didn't shake in the telling, but she knew what agony it cost him to re-live those events.

"We got the fire brigade, tried to reach them both, of course, but it was useless." His voice was tired-sounding, on one note. "At the enquiry they put it down to pilot error. There was nothing said but a lot implied that bigshot producers were prone to take risks in order to achieve realism. That didn't help, neither did the publicity. When the enquiries were all over, I just went into hiding. Whatever was said I *did* blame myself. I hadn't had that plane checked before take-off. I'd simply trusted to Glen Charles's word, and he had been in a right state to say nothing of what Mandy told him when she was up there. I'd a right to feel aggrieved, not to cost two people their lives."

"So you decided you'd not produce again, in the same way I told myself I couldn't come here, where Ken had done so much. This pageant forced reality back on both of us."

"Yes. I went to stay with Don for a while. He seemed the only person I could rely on to let me wallow on in my own misery. He'd promised Ted he'd produce this pageant but the day before he was due to come to Stretton he was offered a job in Canada as principal of a new Mime and Drama College. They wanted him, for an interview and it was either then or they'd pass him over. I told him he must go and he asked me to come in his place. At first I said no, but he'd been good to me and I liked Ted and — "

"You just slipped into using Don's name?"

"It seemed harmless enough and the Press had been plaguing me since the accident. Some of the Sundays had run lurid accounts of Mandy's career and death and — "

"Ted agreed to go along with the idea."

"I think he thought it might prove my cure."

"As Harry did when he sent me here."

"Something like that."

"And Claire?"

"Claire's been trying to get me for weeks. She discovered that Glen had been high on L.S.D. and he probably was dosed up before he took off. She had suspicions that Mandy had been experimenting with him. The management of the hotel she'd stayed at complained of a great deal of noise and damage to the suite. Bless her,

Claire thought if I knew that I'd stop blaming myself for what had happened. She probably believed that I'd face the performance more confidently if I knew beforehand, except that she got locked in."

Jennifer drew a swift breath. "I locked her in deliberately. I thought she would interfere and — did she tell you?"

"No, but I guessed it hadn't been an accident. Jenny?"

"Yes?"

"You've known for some time, haven't you that I wasn't Don Wilson?"

"Yes. Mrs. Charlesworth said things and I heard Don didn't ride well and then I found the photograph of Don without his front teeth and — "

"That?" He gave a hoot of laughter. "I should have known after Norris clouted me. Don was always grousing about those teeth. Why didn't you accuse me?"

"I thought — well, I wasn't sure — why — "

"You didn't think I was involved in

anything criminal?" He drew back to stare at her in the deepening gloom. "You *did*. You thought I might have kidnapped Chris Prevot."

"Well, Ann lost a hypo at Ted's and — "

"You've got more imagination than the writers I have on the set. Oh, my poor Jenny, then when you saw Claire you jumped to the conclusion I was married."

"I didn't know you were not. You still hadn't. 'declared yourself' as they say in historical novels."

He sobered again. "I should have told you the moment I knew I cared for you."

"How — how long ago was that?"

"The day I saw you here at the gate and we talked, then when we rode together — I think full realisation came when Cliff hit me and I knew I had a rival."

"I think I began to love you, too, at the same moment."

His eyes twinkled, "From the time I

stopped thinking of your Richard as a murderer?"

"You're teasing me again." She wriggled uncomfortably on the gate. "But do you — "

"What? Think he was a murderer? No, I doubt it. From what I've read it wasn't in his nature. He could be ruthless but he wasn't stupid and that murder would have been. It would have caused him more embarrassment than it helped. I've decided to make a film about him. After the considerable interest shown here in the pageant it was inevitable that I'd be obsessed with the idea. I'm even toying with the thought of playing the lead part myself."

"Then you're going back to work?"

"Yes. I had to sort out my complexes I think that's why it was easy to fall into the character of Ted's nephew. No-one expected anything remarkable of him. It wasn't easy facing the responsibility. I'd built up a mental block. I couldn't stop seeing that bi-plane go up in flames. I was terrified for the safety of the children — literally terrified."

"That's why you insisted on playing Richard yourself. You were afraid that Cliff might be injured in that final charge."

"He admitted that he was an inexperienced horseman, then, as it fell out, it was young Pete who was injured."

She nodded thoughtfully.

"Was Mandy a little like Sue Greenacre?"

"Why do you ask that? Not to look at, no, not in the slightest but she was spoilt and men flocked round to admire constantly. I suppose, subconsciously, I fused the two images in my mind. You think I was hard on Sue."

"You seemed convinced that we were all worrying unnecessarily."

"Afterwards it dawned on me that she might have been harmed. That's why I was so anxious to find those men." He laughed. "I'm not usually such a quixotic fool as to risk my neck, not that I was in any real danger."

He jumped down and held out his arms to assist her, holding her close to his heart.

"Now I know where I'm going and I'm a whole man again, I can ask you, Jenny. Will you be my wife?"

She lifted her face to his. "Yes, Don, I love you only — "

"Only?"

"I don't think I shall be a good hostess or mix well with the smart 'in' crowd or — "

"You'll be just what I need, Jenny. I don't want to wait. When I fly to the States I want you with me."

"I'll come. I'll be there whenever you need me, but — "

"Still 'buts'?" He nuzzled her hair gently. "What's wrong now?"

"It's going to be so awkward. I'll never get used to calling you anything but 'Don'."

He chuckled. "I don't think the problem is as great as you think."

"I don't understand."

"While I adopted 'Guy Lander' as my professional name, it happened to be a nickname which stuck, my real name, *first* name, happens to be — Richard."

"Oh, no." They stared at each other, then broke into sudden laughter, then he took her hand to lead her back to the village.

THE END